What

the Old-timer

Said. . . .

The celebrated Professor Foley* tells

*Allen R. Foley,

Professor Emeritus of American History,

Dartmouth College

What

the Old-timer Said

—*and Then Some!*—

to the feller from down-country,

and even to his neighbor

(when he had it coming)

Illustrated by John Devaney

The Stephen Greene Press

Brattleboro, Vermont

Lexington, Massachusetts

PUBLISHED SEPTEMBER 1983
Second printing December 1983

This book is manufactured in the United States of America. It is published by The Stephen Greene Press, Fessenden Road, Brattleboro, Vermont 05301.

Library of Congress Cataloging in Publication Data

Foley, Allen R. (Allen Richard), 1898-
   What the old-timer said (and then some!)

   "Originally published as What the old-timer said and
The old-timer talks back"— T.p. verso.
   1. American wit and humor—Vermont. I. Foley,
Allen R. (Allen Richard), 1898-   More snappers,
whoppers, japes, and drolleries, as the old-timer talks
back. 1983. II. title.
PN6162.F55   1983   818'.5402   83-11635
ISBN 0-8289-0516-9 (pbk.)

Contents

Dorrance

About thirty years ago I moved from New Hampshire near Dartmouth College, where I was teaching American history, across the Connecticut River to Norwich, Vermont. Soon I began to roam the back-country and visit with local people of all ages and walks of life, collecting quips and yarns from them and about them. This little book is a fair sampling of the stories I have heard and passed along in my talks over the years, and while I can't footnote all of them, some of the best I can vouch for, and all of them I certainly heard in Vermont.

*   *

People who once have known the lure and the lift of the Green Mountain State never seem to forget the attitudes engendered there, or the people who epitomize them. Terseness and dryness—"dry" is still high praise given for someone's humor—independence, thrift and emotional restraint are perhaps the hallmarks of this part of the North Country. Of course none is strictly unique to Vermont, but seemingly each is incised a little more deeply for being set there.

In my wanderings and gatherings I made some of my life's most rewarding friendships, and perhaps foremost among them was Dorrance Sargent (1882–1967), tenth generation American and third generation son of Norwich.

He was a little heavy for a Vermonter—he weighed over two hundred pounds—but in most other respects he seemed to qualify. In speech and manner and dress, in attitude toward debts and taxes and pious patriots, in independence of spirit, a friendly way with animals and a wry sense of humor: in such ways as these Dorrance qualified as a good old-fashioned Vermonter—and a "character" to boot.

I have heard Dorrance remark more than once, when referring to friends and neighbors, "We don't visit enough"; and though he and Henry David Thoreau might not appear to be very much of a piece, Dorrance, like the sage of Walden Pond, certainly never counted that time lost which is used in visiting—or sitting and reflecting—or just sitting. It was this, in fact, that first attracted me to him—this, and stories told me by a neighbor who kept his horse in the Sargent barn and said he had learned a lot from Dorrance.

In fact, there are many stories I've heard from Dorrance and about Dorrance. One of them dates back to the time when he was a Selectman in Norwich, a position which he filled for at least a dozen years. It seemed that a back-hill farmer in the town had suffered loss by the deer eating his buckwheat, but because he had not filed the proper sort of formal complaint by letter with the Selectmen, he had not been able to recover any damages. The next year he vowed he'd be smarter, and when the deer started eating his bean vines,

he appeared at Dorrance's house in the village with his letter in his hand.

"There, Dorrance," he announced. "Last year I didn't get nothing, but this year I was ready for those deer. Here's the letter you said I had to write." "All right," said Dorrance. "But according to the law I have to go and examine the damage and see if in my opinion you deserve payment. If I think you do, I report it to the game warden."

So Dorrance went with the farmer and found that where the deer had eaten the leaves off the bean plants, the beans were ripening well, but where they hadn't eaten the leaves, the beans didn't seem to be coming along at all.

Said Dorrance, after due deliberation: "Don't appear to me that the deer have done you any harm. Fact is, they seem to have done you good. Don't know but what we ought to charge for their services."

"Maybe you're right," agreed the farmer. "Give me back my letter."

Dorrance denied that he was much of a trader, but he had been known to be party to an exchange of horses —he'd even swapped a farm or two—and was usually ready to dicker about anything from a cow to a bantam rooster. He liked to recall the time some years ago when a neighbor from up on the hill came round with a calf

he wanted to sell and the time-honored steps in bargaining began.

"How much will you give?"

"How much will you take?"

"God, I don't know."

"I want to finish my haying first."

"I don't need to sell that bad."

"Well, I don't know as I want the critter anyhow."

You know the way such exchange runs on—back and forth like a shuttle. Both parties realize like as not that in due time the deal will be closed, and about how it will be closed; but neither wants to hurry. Each thinks he sees some advantage in playing for time, so whenever the gap seems to be closing a little fast, one or the other will interpose a diversionary remark. At one point, for instance, Dorrance had commented on the fact that Obadiah was driving a different horse, and Obadiah had allowed as how his uncle had gone south for the winter and asked him to keep the horse. Some time later when another diversionary remark seemed in order, Dorrance had returned to the subject of the uncle who'd gone south.

"How's your uncle liking it down in Florida?" asked Dorrance.

"Oh, he didn't go to Florida," said Obadiah. "He went downriver to Vernon."

And Dorrance liked to tell how Obadiah, after debating it for weeks, decided to drive way down south to Vernon to see his uncle: "If I get too tired on the trip," Obadiah declared, "I'll pull off the road and go to sleep."

"You'd have thought," said Dorrance, "that 'stead of being about eighty miles it was three hundred. But he made it all right—and got back, too."

It was another friend of Dorrance's, according to his tell, who had been married for thirty years and all that time had always compared his wife's cooking with his mother's, and not in his wife's favor. One Thanksgiving the wife thought she would do the very best she knew and see if for once her meal wouldn't be as good as his mother's.

Her husband ate with relish, and after he was all done she remarked, "Well, you seemed to like that meal well enough."

The husband thought quite a while, running over the major items in his mind.

"'Twas good," he allowed at last. "The turkey was roasted just right and the dressing was well seasoned. The mashed potato was smooth and good. The other vegetables was done just the way I like them, and even the pie and the pudding was good. But the gravy—that gravy . . . well, Mother's gravy always had lumps in it."

❈   ❈

One Monday night Dorrance and his wife, Mina, were driving home downriver on U.S. Route 5 from the weekly cattle auction at East Thetford. Dorrance was driving his 1941 Chevrolet panel truck at about his usual speed of twenty miles an hour, with now and then acceleration to twenty-five. At a place where the tracks of the Passumpsic Division of the Boston & Maine run parallel to the road a freight train came along, going Dorrance's way, and passed him. Dorrance said he heard a whistle and remarked to Mina that they changed the whistles on those darn diesels so often a feller couldn't ever keep track of them. After the train was pulling on ahead of him he still heard the whistle.

"Then," said he, "I looked in my looking glass and saw a State Police car behind me. He seemed to be in a hurry, so I pulled over and let him pass.

"As he passed me he started blinking that red light of his so I pulled up and stopped. The officer came back to me and says, 'You didn't pay much attention to a sireen, did you?'

" 'I didn't hear a sireen. Thought 'twas the whistle on that diesel that went by. Said to Mina here, how they change those darn whistles so often a fellow can't keep track of them nohow.'

" 'Never mind that,' said the officer. 'You're driving

too slow, Mister. I'll have to see your driver's license.'

" 'Well,' I told him, 'it's a good thing you asked for that *this* week rather than last. I tucked it away, some time ago, when I was changing my clothes and hadn't been able to find it for a month, but this week I found it and I got it right here in my pocket.' "

The license was examined and found to be in order, and then the officer reminded Dorrance again that they couldn't have cars driving so slow on a main road and holding up traffic.

" 'I don't see that I was holding up traffic,' Dorrance told him. 'You was the only fellow being held up, and I pulled over and let you by. I don't know about this going too slow. I wonder what the law is. Guess I'll have to read up on that.

" 'And you talk about going too slow. Now, I've got a horse up to the barn—and a buggy—and if you think I'm going too slow, I can hitch up the horse and see what you think then. Guess I've got a right to ride on the road, ain't I? And if that's not slow enough I've been known to drive a yoke of oxen down to White River. How's *that* seem to you?' "

The officer evidently figured Dorrance was something of a local character and let him go his way.

"But I wasn't quite satisfied in my mind," Dorrance told me, "and next evening I read in a law book for most an hour's time, but I couldn't seem to find what I wanted. So I says to myself, the next time I go down to White River to get stale bread from the bakery for my cattle I'm going across the street to the State Police and find out what the rule is.

"Well, the next time we went down to White River I said to Mina, 'When I get this car parked I'm going across the street to the State Police offices and find out what the law is.'

"So I went across the street, but hang it, they had moved. It was too far to walk over to the new place, so I ain't found out yet. But I intend to look into that."

*　　*

"Times change and we change with them!" says the Latin tag. Of course we do—we are all bound to change somewhat. But the significant thing is that in different areas and different individuals the rate of change varies greatly. Dorrance Sargent was one of those folks whose rate of change was very slow. One could glimpse in him, it seemed, a living picture of older days and ways.

Quick & Dry

If you mix at all with the old-timers I know, it won't be very long before you meet up with their proclivity to make the terse, dry comment or retort. And if it sets you back a bit you must realize that such is both their intention and their pleasure. It's a harmless game, which doesn't cost anybody anything and can be an unending source of amusement regardless of time or place or weather.

Nor do they play it only on visiting strangers and summer people and city folks: they also, to keep in practice, play it on each other. Thus it becomes part of their accepted way of life—so much so, that certain comebacks seem to be treasured as almost automatic responses to particular stimuli. For instance:

An old Thetford farm family was gathered around the kitchen table to fill out the insurance forms for the farmer, who had fallen off the barn roof, broken his neck and died. They recorded all the facts as best they could—date and hour and nature of the accident, and so on—and finally under the heading *Remarks* solemnly wrote: "He didn't make none."

A neighbor told me the story of the oldster who was accosted by a traveling evangelist. "Excuse me, my friend—have you found Jesus?" the preacher began. "God," said the old man, "I didn't know he was lost."

On first encounter, at least, people from down-country are apt to find the natives somewhat "different" and sometimes "very strange." When such a visitor commented to an old Vermonter that there seemed to be a lot of very peculiar people around he agreed: "Yes, there are; but most of them are gone by the middle of September."

A leading citizen of Royalton was sitting on his porch in the cool of the evening when a tourist from New Jersey paused to chat. "Have you lived here all your life?" the stranger asked. "Not yet," was the low-pitched reply.

A farmer and his hired hand were by the road when a motorist inquired if he was on the right road for Jericho Center, and the farmer gave affirmative reply. After he had driven on the hired man remarked, "You didn't tell him the bridge was out." "Nope," said the farmer. "He didn't ask."

Sometimes I rib my fellow legislators by reporting the discussion between two old boys at a political rally where a candidate for office was going on at great length. One of them, a bit hard of hearing, asked his friend, "What's he talking about?" And received the precis: "He don't say."

Yankees from the hill-country are noted for responding to questions by asking one of their own, as epitomized in the exchange: "How's your wife?" a neighbor inquired. "Compared to what?" was the canny counterquery.

A tourist inquired of an old-timer the way to Wheelock and was told, "Well, Mister, if I was going to Wheelock I'd be damned if I'd start from here."

And Walter Piston, the great musician and composer at Harvard, tells of taking a rather back-roads route from a concert at Tanglewood in the Berkshires to Hanover, New Hampshire, for an engagement at Hopkins Center and coming to a fork that had signs pointing in both directions saying *White River Junction*. "Does it make any difference," he inquired of an old-timer standing near by, "which road I take to White River?" If not enlightened, Walter was duly impressed by the answer: "Not to me it don't."

I recently overheard Whit Hicks of Dan and Whit's store in Norwich make reply to a summer resident who had been giving a long order over the phone.

She had inquired (he told me): "Mr. Hicks, I don't hear anything—are you still there?"

"Yep," replied Whit; "I write quiet."

In the old days Dartmouth's Professor Fred Parker Emery, '87, used to ride his horse in Vermont, and one day, over beyond Beaver Meadow, he came upon a lonely farm and reined up to visit with the old native standing in the barnyard.

"Aren't you sometimes lonely here?" inquired the Professor.

"Don't know what you're talking about," was the reply.

Said Professor Emery, somewhat on the defensive, "I just thought sometimes you might wish you were nearer to the center of things."

"Mister," was the rather deliberate rejoinder, "I'm exactly five miles from Norwich village. I'm exactly five miles from Strafford. I'm exactly one hundred fifty miles from Boston and one hundred fifty miles from Montreal. Don't see how a feller could be much nearer to the center of things."

More recently another Dartmouth professor—of German background and rather Prussian characteristics—rode up to the old Norwich store, now made into apartments, dismounted, and said brusquely to an old native sitting on the steps, "Watch my horse!"

Coming out a few minutes later he discovered that

his horse was missing. Said the professor, this time in a sharp and critical tone, "I thought I told you to watch my horse."

"I did," said the old man, pointing. "Just going 'round that corner yonder."

A nurse at the Waterbury State Hospital was in the yard walking a couple of patients who were recovering from mental problems. A passing bird dropped a calling card on the bald head of one, and the nurse, solicitous for his emotional balance, told him not to worry—"just stay right here and I'll go in the building and bring a piece of toilet paper."

When she had disappeared the old man said to his companion, "Ain't she a damn fool. That bird'll be a quarter a mile away 'fore she gets back."

In the summer of 1968 two middle-aged ladies from New York bought a place in northern Vermont with the intention of making it their year-round home. They were naturally apprehensive about their first winter in the North Country, and in the fall one of them asked a nearby farmer what kind of a winter it was going to be.

"Oh," the old-timer reassured them, "it's going to be a good winter."

They didn't happen to encounter that neighbor until about the first of March in 1969, after a winter with a very heavy fall of snow, and gently reproved him with the comment, "We thought you said it was going to be a good winter."

"I did," he replied. "What's been the matter with it?"

"Why, my goodness, look at all this snow!"

"God," retorted the old farmer, "I never told you it wan't going to *snow*."

A Vermonter had bought an old, run-down farm and had worked very hard getting it back in good operating condition. When it was back in pretty good working shape the local minister happened to stop by for a call. He congratulated the farmer on the results of his labors, remarking that it was wonderful what God and man could do when working together.

"Ayeh," allowed the farmer, "p'raps it is. But you should have seen this place when God was running it alone."

It may have been this same minister who had persuaded his congregation to redecorate the interior of the church and at a church meeting was complimenting the flock on a job well done. He then pointed out that just one thing more was needed to make the sanctuary a place of real beauty. He said he had spoken to the Board of Deacons about a new chandelier, and wondered what the decision would be. The chairman of the board rose slowly to his feet and reported as follows:

"I don't think the board will recommend that,

Reverend, and for three reasons. In the first place none of us could spell it. In the second place if we got one there's nobody could play it. And in the third place what this church really needs is better light."

And then there's the retort to the hill-country preacher who had his congregation all worked up about the glories of Heaven and the terrors of Hell and finally invited to stand all those who wanted to go to Heaven, "where there would be no more sorrow nor crying nor pain, and no more suffering." After long urging he had all the congregation on their feet except for a nice little old lady in the front pew.

"What's the matter with you, Aunt Mary, don't you want to go to Heaven?"

And Aunt Mary placidly replied, "Not today. I got company."

A minister went 'way back in the hills to substitute at a service at which one man proved to be the entire congregation. The preacher asked him if he thought they should go on with the service.

He thought awhile and then replied, "Well, Reverend, if I put some hay in the wagon and go down to the pasture to feed the cows and only one cow shows up, I feed her."

So the good brother went through most of the service, including a full-length sermon. Afterwards he

asked the lone member of the congregation what he
thought of it.

"Well, Reverend, I'll tell you. If I put some hay in
the wagon and go down to the pasture to feed the cows
and only one cow shows up I don't give her the whole
damn load."

Every old-timer knows there's more than one way to skin a cat, and I like especially the story of how the Reverend James Converse, for many years pastor of the lovely church in Weathersfield Center, forestalled a demonstration of rebellion by his flock.

It seems that a number of parishioners considered him too authoritarian, and finally the members of the choir announced they'd take their regular places on the coming Sunday, but they'd refuse to take part in the singing. The threatened strike was noised abroad, and on Sunday the church was filled to overflowing with folks anxious to see how the Reverend would cope.

He didn't keep them waiting, but hauled the disaffected choir into line with his opening announcement:

"Let us open the service by singing Hymn Twenty-four, 'Come we who love the Lord.' We will begin with the second verse, which starts, 'Let those refuse to sing, who never knew their Lord / But children of the Heavenly King should speak their joy abroad.' "

I was still teaching at Dartmouth when a good friend, an elderly farmer from Caledonia County, came to visit me during our famous Winter Carnival. He hadn't been in Hanover for forty years and was curious to see all the changes.

We stood on Main Street watching the ebb and flow of the carnival throng and all the lovely girls in ski outfits, including stretch pants. As three very attractive specimens went by my farmer friend remarked, "Those I suppose be some of the carnival babes."

"Yes," I replied, "I suppose they be."

Said he, "I suppose the boys think they've got 'bout everything."

"Yes," said I. "At any rate they live in hope, for they spend good money to have them here."

As we watched them move away my Caledonian friend, without taking his eyes from the girls, continued, "Well, there's one thing I can tell you they ain't got enough of."

From my angle I thought they had too much of it and I was interested to get his slant. "What's that?" I asked.

"Hindsight," said he.

I have heard tell of the New Yorker who had a Great Dane on a leash and tried to board a bus in Vermont. The driver opened the bus door and, looking out at the pair, said: "You can't get on this bus."

"Why can't I get on the bus?" snapped the New Yorker.

"No dogs allowed on this bus," countered the driver.

To which the New Yorker retorted, not with the greatest display of understanding and courtesy, "OK, you know what you can do with your damned bus."

Equal to the occasion, the driver replied, "You do the same with your dog and you can get on."

Years ago in Barnet I encountered three local farmers sitting on the steps of an old country store. I was new at the game and probably didn't make quite the right approach. At any rate I couldn't seem to get a word out of them; their lips seemed to be hermetically sealed. Finally, slightly irritated, I inquired if there was a law in that town against talking. At that, one of the old gentlemen made this reply:

"No, there's no law in this town 'gainst talking but we aim to keep our mouths shut unless we're damn sure we can improve on the silence!"

✳ ✳

A more sophisticated Vermont friend of mine used to like to make his own additions to the Beatitudes, and one of his favorite ones would have found approval in Barnet: "Blessed is the man who having nothing to say abstains from giving wordy evidence of the fact."

A story current in Stowe in the old days concerned a city lady who rented a place for the summer, and asked a native who was sort of her Man Friday what she should do about her garbage, which was perhaps a little more nutritious in those days. He told her that most of the folks around there kept a pig; she liked the idea and he agreed to get her a small one. Everything worked out well, and during the summer the little pig grew to greater size. In September she asked what she should do with the pig, and the conversation is reported to have gone like this:

"I can't take my nice piggy home with me. What do I do with it?"

"Sell it," replied her helper.

"What should I get for it?" she asked. "I paid ten dollars for it, you remember. But of course I've had the use of it all summer. Would five dollars be fair enough?"

"Ayeh," said the Vermonter. "Fair enough."

A lady from Park Avenue visited a fox farm near
Bennington back in the days when we had farmers who
raised foxes for their pelts. She exclaimed over one
particular fox, "Oh, such a beautiful animal, such a
charming creature! How many pelts do you get annually
from each fox?"

"Well," said the farmer, "I'll tell you, ma'am—
usually not more than two. If you skin 'em more than
twice a year it makes 'em damn nervous."

*   *

One of my Norwich neighbors, who lives up at the
dead end of Dutton Hill Road, had gone to the mill for
grain on a day in spring when the road was deep in mud.
While he was gone he telephoned his sister, and her first
question was, "Are you stuck, Paul?"

"Nope," was Paul's slow reply. "But if I tried to get
out I might be."

Another April, Paul found a feller from down-country who had obviously not displayed any great skill as a driver, had got mired, and was standing beside his car condemning the road to hell and back. Paul approached on foot, assessed the situation, and pronounced:

"I wouldn't put all the blame on the rud."

Our local road commissioner told me of stopping in Beaver Meadow to visit with an old bachelor who lived alone in squalor but who, at the urging of his friends, had had a telephone installed. The phone was ringing insistently—one long and three short—and Charlie asked him, "Ain't that your ring?"

The old-timer guessed it was, whereupon Charlie said, "Then why don't you answer the damn thing?"

"Charlie," came the deliberate reply, "I had that phone put in for *my* convenience."

Like most human beings the hill-country Yankees enjoy giving free advice, and sometimes manage to have their fun while doing so—whether the recipient be a neighbor or a visitor from outside.

In a flood on the Connecticut years ago the house of a relatively prosperous Vermonter in a small upper-valley town was washed downstream with the owner riding on the roof. Happily he was rescued by a boy who managed to get him off in his boat. When things had quieted down the rescued man was discussing with some of his cronies in the village store what reward he should give the boy to show his gratitude.

One friend suggested a hundred dollars, another that he help the boy go on to school, and so on around the circle until it was the turn of an old codger who suggested quietly: "You should've made your terms in advance."

An old gentleman who used to live alone on U.S. 5 just a little above Hartland village displayed in front of his house one summer a sign which said *Poison Ivy for Sale*. A person who stopped to inquire what this was all about received a reply that went something like this:

"Well, one of my neighbors up the road a piece—name's Bill—advertised beagle pups for sale. Another one named Gladys has gladiolas. And Mildred has maple syrup. They seem to get a lot of people stopping so I thought I'd try. Didn't have much to offer 'cept a lot of poison ivy out back, so I put up that sign.

"I ain't sold none yet but I do get the most interesting people dropping by. Made a whole new life for me!"

A New York lawyer who has a summer place in the Green Mountains wrote me about a very helpful piece of advice he had recently from a neighbor.

The lawyer was busy with the many chores in closing his place for the winter but interrupted his work to say goodbye to his neighbor at a time he thought appropriate for the farmer's schedule. It turned out, as it sometimes does with supposedly taciturn denizens of the hill-country, that his neighbor wanted to talk, and after some exchange the lawyer said, "I'm sorry but I've got to go along. Have a hundred things to do."

"You've got a *hundred* things to do?"

"Well, perhaps not quite," the New Yorker replied, "but it seems like that many."

"Let me give you a piece of advice," said the Vermonter. "Do 'em *one at a time*."

The lawyer told me he has put that message on a card on his desk in the city, and when things pile up and the going gets tough he pictures his friend—and more calmly tackles his assignments "one at a time."

Land values in Vermont have risen tremendously in recent years and there's hardly a man, woman or child who isn't aware of this fact, but one of my old friends told me of the sharp operator from the city who thought that, if he went far back in the country, he might pick up some good land at a very favorable price. He cruised around until he came on a sightly hill-farm 'way back from nowhere, accosted the farmer, and after some conversation said, "I'd like to buy about five hundred dollar's worth of land from you."

"Good," said the old farmer, "that's very good. Go fetch your wheelbarrow and I'll fill it up for you."

A schoolboy in Corinth told me that last October he had recited his adapted version of the old jingle:

> As I was sitting in a shady nook,
> Along beside a babbling brook,
> I saw a lovely little lass
> Standing in water up to her knees.

When I remarked that he didn't seem to have the right rhyme he answered:

"That's what the teacher said, but I told her you had to remember we've had a helluva dry fall."

The Green Mountain folk keep surprisingly up to date on general affairs, and I heard recently about a conversation concerning the population explosion.

"Ain't it terrible," said one old-timer. "They tell me that by the year 2000 there'll be standing room only."

"Well," said the other, "that ought to slow 'em down a little."

A group of old-timers were sitting quietly on the steps of the village store when a movement on the hill road opposite the store caused them to look up that way. A heavy-set neighbor from up on the hill was coming down toward the village, straight out and full tilt. After a while one of the watchers broke the silence.

"Here comes old Asa," he remarked, "too goddam lazy to hold back!"

One time Robert Frost was going trout fishing with two friends from Ripton. One reported at the hour agreed upon but the other, named Ira Dow, was very late in arriving.

While they waited for Ira (generally pronounced I-ree in Vermont) the other friend explained to Frost: "That Iree Dow—you know, he's as much slower than stock-still as stock-still is slower than greased lightning."

A judge was trying to get a jury panel lined up when the sheriff came in with a back-country farmer who said he couldn't serve. The farmer was embarrassed and allowed as how his wife was about to become pregnant. The sheriff explained to the judge that what the gentleman meant was that his wife was about to be confined.

Whereupon the State's Attorney, sitting in the corner with his chair tipped back against the wall, put in his penny's worth: "Whichever way it is, Your Honor, I kinda think he ought to be there."

Inquiries about directions are as numerous in the North Country as elsewhere, and afford the interested native a ready chance to play the game.

A motorist pulled up and hollered to a young Vermonter, "Hi, Bub, is this the way to Cabot?"

Replied the chap, "What makes you think my name is Bub?"

"Oh, I just guessed it," answered the stranger.

"Well, why don't you guess the way to Cabot?"

One fine summer day a stranger stopped his car at a barnyard to inquire the way to East Barnard. The farmer gave him rather elaborate and detailed directions. The stranger followed them carefully and about a half-

hour later found himself back in the same barnyard. Somewhat irate he got out of his car and walked over to the farmer with the intention of letting him know what he thought of him.

"Damn it!" he shouted, "I asked the way to East Barnard. I followed your directions and here I am right back where I started from."

"That's good," said the farmer. "That's good. I wanted to find out first if you was capable of following directions. Now I can tell you how to get to East Barnard."

A city visitor was asking an old Green Mountain man how to get to a certain Methodist church back up in the hills.

"Well now, I'll tell you," said the native. "You go straight ahead on this rud. 'Bout a mile down take the right fork, and after quite a piece you'll come to an iron bridge. Now 'bout a half-mile before you come to that bridge you want to take a sharp left turn and you'll find the church up at the top of the hill."

When a storekeeper in Wardsboro asked a friend "How's your wife?" He was told that she wasn't too well, that in fact she was home in bed with arthritis.

"Arthuritis," mused the storekeeper, "Arthuritis . . . I know Fred Itis and Joe Itis, but God, I guess I don't know Arthur Itis."

They tell in Peacham about the distinguished Harvard professor who one summer day some years ago bent over the little window in the post office and inquired of the postmistress, "Do you know any farms for sale around here?"

Her terse reply was, "Don't know of any that ain't."

She was not completely accurate perhaps, but I suppose even in Peacham every man has his price.

I have been Moderator of the Town of Norwich since 1957, and have found sometimes that borrowing from the Vermonters' unexpected retorts eases a tense situation and keeps the meeting moving. On one occasion I had made a comment after a vote and one good citizen spoke up, "Mr. Moderator, I am not sure I agree with your last remark."

It was in my opinion not a matter of great moment and I answered him quickly: "Doctor, you haven't heard my *last* remark!"

The crowd laughed, the Doctor laughed, and the meeting moved peacefully to the next article in the Warning.

And now that we are back home in Norwich I should include one other illustration involving that family mentioned earlier who live at the dead end of the Dutton Hill Road. Some years ago the two brothers—Paul and Fred—were looking at an unfamiliar piece of farm equipment at the World's Fair at Tunbridge. "What's that?" asked Fred.

"Looks like some sort of a separator," Paul decided.

"Don't look like a separator to me," replied Fred.

"You just wait around," said Paul, "and you'll see it separate some damn fool from his money."

A real old-timer in Norwich had agreed to give a boy lessons on the church organ from one to two o'clock on Sunday afternoons. The boy lived next door to the church and his mother had invited the organist—none other than the Fred just mentioned—to have the Sunday noon meal with the family and thus save Fred the trip home up on Dutton Hill and coming back at one o'clock. It so happened that to make it easy for the lady of the house the Sunday noon meal was always clam chowder. This went on pleasantly for some time, and then the lessons were dropped.

Months later, on learning that Fred had to come back to the village at one o'clock on that particular Sunday, the mother invited Fred to renew old times and have clam chowder with them. Fred's sister, Abbie, happened to overhear the conversation and remarked, "Fred doesn't like clam chowder."

"Why didn't you tell me that?" the mother asked Fred.

"Well," said Fred, "you can even get used to hangin' if you hang long enough."

A Princeton professor who summered at Caspian Lake in Greensboro went walking and stopped to visit with an eighty-five-year-old farmer who lived in the area. Learning that the old man had five sons who had farms in the neighborhood, he congratulated the farmer and added, "It must be a great satisfaction to you to have such a fine family, and all living near you."

"Yes," said the old man, "it is. I had six boys and I raised every one of them 'cept one who died when he was sixty."

A New York family that had spent summers in Vermont decided in retirement to try staying year round. When winter came, a native farmer who lived some distance up the road started going by early every morning with a pair of horses pulling a long, heavy chain behind them.

After a few mornings curiosity got the better of our city friends and the man of the house went out to the road to inquire what was going on.

"Why do you drag that heavy chain along every morning?" he asked.

Countered the Vermonter: "Did you ever hear of anybody trying to push a chain?"

And many a village has a storekeeper like the one in Burke who was out of a certain popular item and was asked if he'd have it in stock before long.

"Nope," he replied.

"Why not?" the customer wanted to know.

"Moves too damn fast."

An elderly man from up Strafford way has from time to time been a great help to a neighbor of mine in her yard and garden. She hadn't seen him for quite a spell and then there he was at the door—his tall, spare frame, his craggy face with just a faint trace of a smile. "My, my,"

she said. "Am I glad to see you. It's been quite a while. How are things?"

His reply carried the essence of Vermont-ness: "No worse."

During World War II Jones & Lamson of Springfield, Vermont, had large contracts with the U.S. Navy and on one occasion a Navy inspection team, consisting of an admiral, three captains, and a lieutenant came to Springfield on an official visit. The Navy people were taken on tour of the plant by a W. D. Woolson, who was head man for J&L at the time.

In one large room where nearly one hundred men were employed, the admiral, with booming voice, inquired, "How many men do you have working in this room, Mr. Woolson?"

Mr. Woolson looked around rather slowly before he replied. " 'Bout half," he said.

Independence

If we could get the pollsters to make a survey of the characteristics of Vermonters, I am sure that "independence of spirit" would be high on the list, and probably at the top. To be sure, there are lots of independent-minded people in other parts of the United States and in some other parts of the world, but I doubt if being independent is more deeply indigenous anywhere than in the area of the old Republic of Vermont. The years of that Republic (1777–1791) still influence the native attitudes, as exemplified in the Town of Guilford, hard by the Massachusetts border.

The Revolution ‘had been fought and won the year before the great Ethan Allen marched into the town with his Green Mountain Boys to quell an armed uprising, and thundered: ". . .Unless the inhabitants of Guilford peacefully submit to the authority of Vermont I swear that I will lay it as desolate as Sodom and Gomorrah by God!"

This was in 1782. It was a good many years later that a friend of mine enjoyed describing for me the hill farmer who took what might seem, to a Guilford resident, to be the last logical step: he declared his independence of the town, loaded his musket for bear, and defied the authorities to set foot on his land.

"There," said my friend, "is a cussed good Vermonter for you."

I haven't found as much humor in this area of thought as in some others, for independence of spirit is after all a serious matter. But here follow a few items that may be apropos.

In September of 1941, a few months before Pearl Harbor, the legislature of Vermont got sick and tired of what it regarded as a policy of appeasement being pursued in Washington, and, perhaps recalling the glorious days of the Republic of Vermont, passed a Resolution practically declaring war on Nazi Germany. There was no great stir in Berlin when Hitler learned of this move, and no one seems to know just what force Vermont was prepared to throw against the enemy, but it's the spirit that matters.

A fellow professor at Dartmouth said it reminded him of the mouse which enjoyed a few drops of whiskey and then snarled, "Bring on your damned cat!" But an old Vermont friend of mine wasn't at all bothered by reference to a mouse.

"A mouse," he said, "can be real brave in its way without any whiskey. What I don't like is the false suggestion that Vermonters had to get liquored up to take that independent stand."

There was the experience of the city boy brought by
some Fresh Air type of fund for a few weeks' vacation in
Vermont, where for the first time in his life he discovered a toad. He was fascinated with the little critter and
kept poking it with a stick to see it hop, until a local lad,

who thought the toad was getting tired of such treatment, said, "Leave that tud alone."

"Why should I?" the city kid asked. "It's my toad, ain't it?"

"No," said the other youngster, "in Vermont he's his own tud!"

I was given—as a superior example of the native Vermont traits of (1) disliking hypocritical amenites, (2) hating to be beholden, and (3) reserving the right to speak one's mind—this letter written to a friend of mine. He's in the construction business, and the letter, with a sizable sum enclosed, was sent him by a Bethel resident for whom he had done some work.

July 1, 1950

Mr. Nelson,

Inclosed find check as per bill. Your charge and services were both very unsatisfactory.

Yours truly, *etc.*

Then there was a summer resident near Woodstock who decided to make his place over for year-round residence and also decided, maybe a little late in the day, that he should be on more friendly terms with the native farmers who lived near him. Walking down the road one beautiful autumn day he met one of his neighbors and, living up to his resolve to be democratic, greeted him.

"Good morning, Mr. ——," he said. "Good morning. And how are you, my good man, on this beautiful October morning?"

"None of your damn business," replied Mr. ——, and then added: "And I wouldn't tell you that much if you weren't a neighbor of mine."

I heard up in the Northeast Kingdom of an old-timer in Lyndonville, I think it was, who sat down one evening by the lamp to fill out a government form which was almost overdue. Like many of us under similar circumstances the old man was not in a pleasant or co-operative frame of mind to start with, and staring him in the face at the head of a box at the top righthand corner of the printed form were the words in bold type: DO NOT WRITE HERE.

Before going any further the old gentleman took a firm grip on his pen and wrote in the box, in equally bold letters, I WRITE WHERE I GODDAM PLEASE.

Nowadays, even though Vermont is on the march to move ahead in education, transportation, industry, and all the other social and economic areas, in some notable ways it remains an island in an expanding megalopolis. And one of the things that makes it such an interesting island can be illustrated by a rock-ribbed native in Fairlee.

"I imagine you've seen a lot of great changes in your lifetime," a city visitor commented.

"Yes," replied the old boy, "sure have. And I've been a-gin every damn one of 'em."

Thrift

About as deep-seated among older natives of the Green Mountains as the spirit of independence is the recognition of the importance—aye, the necessity—of not just preaching, but actively practicing, thrift. This sentiment holds equally true for shrewd business dealing.

A favorite story concerns the farmer who went into the little bank in Chelsea and asked if he could borrow some money. When asked how much he wanted to borrow, he indicated he'd like " 'bout a dollar." The banker expressed some surprise at the smallness of the amount but agreed to the deal, explaining that of course the bank would have to have some security. The farmer said he had in his pocket a $1,000 government bond; the banker agreed that it would be adequate coverage for such a loan. As for interest, 6 percent would be the charge. The farmer allowed as how he would like to pay in advance, so he put down the bond and the six cents, took the dollar and went his way.

A year later he asked to renew the loan, and paid another six cents in advance. The year after that, when he again requested renewal, the banker said, "It's very peculiar that you, with this thousand-dollar bond, keep renewing this one-dollar loan."

"Well, it's damn peculiar," said the farmer, "that you, being a banker, ain't figured this out. I was paying five dollars a year for a lock box to keep my bond. Now I've found a way to keep it safe for six cents."

And although it's rather a long tale I must include my "bottle" story. On some of my return engagements I've been asked to tell it a third or fourth time, and it does have a lot of authentic flavor.

It concerns a shrewd but kindly Vermont doctor who had spent all his practice in a small community and, because of age, was about to take in sail. He was looking for some young doctor to buy him out and consulted the Dean of the Medical School at the University of Vermont. He told his story, warning the Dean that he wanted his people to have a good doctor, and the Dean said he had just the right young man in mind. He sent the young doctor to look over the proposition and the young man found a very comfortable house, including an office and a little lab, a barn and garden and fruit trees, and apparently a very good practice which the old doctor offered to sell, "lock, stock and barrel," at a very attractive price, allowing he knew something about the difficulties of getting started in a practice.

The young doctor was a bit skeptical. Observing what seemed to be a very comfortable living he wondered how this had been accomplished in a small community with a scattered population and no great signs of wealth. He asked the old doctor if his practice had

always been on the up-and-up, or if he'd had to eke out by doing anything not quite—well, not quite . . .

"I'm glad you asked, son," the old doctor said, "and I'll be honest with you. I've never done anything irregular in my practice. It's all a question of thrift and attention to detail.

"I'll give you an illustration. In the summertime the folks around here think they ought to take a vacation, and they'll pack up and go off to the city or the beach and come back a week or two later all tired out and a lot poorer than when they left. My wife and I have never done that. Once in a while we may go to the state medical meeting, but the rest of the time we stay right here. Two or three times during the summer, on some of those lovely days that God gives us here, we close up the house and office, pack a picnic lunch, and go off for the day and gather herbs.

"Come fall, when my wife has to have a fire in the kitchen stove anyway, so it doesn't cost any extra, we put those herbs in a big kettle on the back of the stove

and brew up a good old-fashioned spring tonic. We've always been saving of our bottles and we get them out, wash them and sterilize them, and bottle up that tonic. Then we make up some labels, stick them on the bottles, and put the whole lot away in the closet. And it hasn't cost us a cent!

"Then, in the spring of the year I'll meet one of my patients and I'll say, 'Sue, you don't look too well. What's the matter?'

" 'Doctor,' she'll complain, 'I'm all run down. Never felt so played-out. Got my spring cleaning started but don't know as I'll ever finish it.'

" 'Sue,' I'll say, 'I think what you need is some old-fashioned spring tonic. On the way home why don't you go by the house and tell my wife you want a bottle of our tonic.'

"Now that's only a dollar and a quarter, son, but it's a dollar and a quarter and it's clear profit. A month or so later I'll run into Mrs. —— again and I'll say, 'Why, Sue— how much better you look! That tonic was just what you needed.'

" 'Yes, Doctor,' she'll say, 'never felt better in my life.'

" 'Now, Sue,' I'll say, 'this is just the time in life when you ought to come around for a physical check-up.

Don't wait 'til you've got one foot in the grave and expect the doctor to pull you through. 'Bout your time in life we expect the changes, Sue, and we'll make an appointment right now. And by the way, when you come be sure to bring a specimen.'

"And that's the way, son, we've always got our bottles back."

Back in the days when White River Junction was a great railroad center, a lady came bustling up to the manager of the Old Junction House and demanded, "Are you the proprietor of this hotel?"

"Yes, madam," said he, all polish. "May I help you?"

"I have a complaint," she declared.

"I'm sorry to hear that, madam. What's the nature of your complaint?"

"One of your waitresses just spilled cream over my nice new dress!"

"Now *that*," said the manager, stung to defense of his hostelry, "is a lie, I know from the start, 'cause there's not an ounce of cream in the house."

I spoke once at a Grange meeting in Damon Hall in Hartland. After the meeting a farmer from Tunbridge, the home of the famous World's Fair, told me that in his woodshed attic he had a lot of old books and records which he'd like to have me look at to see if Dartmouth College or the Vermont Historical Society might be interested in having some of them. He'd be glad to donate them. He told me how to get to his farm—first right after going through Tunbridge Plain, then left over a brook, then right by a cemetery, etc.

"Then at the top of a little rise," he said, "you'll see the house. Don't be surprised at the look of the place. Looks a little shabby. We don't paint the outside much. Helps to keep salesmen away and kinda helps on the taxes." And then he added, "But inside you'll find us very comfortable."

I heard a story in Weston about a protest meeting at which the Selectmen were asked to appear and explain why, during a rough winter, the town roads weren't getting more sand and salt. Some of the newer residents were particularly vocal, and after some backing and filling a spokesman for that group got the First Select-man to admit that the town had a good supply of both sand and salt.

"Why don't you use them more freely?" asked the citizen.

"Can't," replied the Selectman.

"But that's the nub of the matter," the spokesman said. "Why can't you?"

"Just can't," said the old-timer. "Sometime we're bound to be needing 'em."

Another take-your-time kind of a yarn has come down from the old days. It involves the son of an old Vermont family who after a long absence came back with his wife to the old place. In the move she had lost a knitting needle, so when our man went to the village to get his horse shod he put an egg in his pocket, contemplating a trade for a new needle. Leaving his horse with the blacksmith he went over to one of the two general stores. The following dialogue ensued:

"Got any knitting needles?"

"Ayeh."

"How much they be?"

"Cent apiece."

"How much for eggs?"

"Twelve cents a dozen."

"Well, I got an egg in my pocket. I'll swap it for a knitting needle."

"That's the retail price for eggs. Can't rightly allow you that much for an egg in trade, but I knew you as a boy, and your father before you, and his father 'fore that, and I'd rather have you trade here than 'cross the road, so I'll swap."

He put the needle down on the counter and took the egg. When the farmer didn't pick up the needle he inquired what the trouble was.

"Well, I'd heard tell that when you got a new customer you usually gave him a noggin of rum."

"Usually I do. 'Course I'm not going to make anything on this deal anyway, but I knew you as a boy, and your father 'fore you and his father 'fore that, and I'd rather not have you trade across the street, so I'll give you a noggin of rum."

After a trip to the back room he put the noggin of rum on the counter; but the farmer didn't take that either.

"Now what's the trouble?"

"Well, I've heard tell that when you gave a new customer a noggin of rum you sometimes dropped a raw egg in it."

"Damn it, I'm certainly not making a penny on this deal as it is, but as I said before I've known all your folks, so as a favor to you I'll break an egg in the rum."

He took the egg the fellow had just brought in and broke it in the noggin. As he did so it appeared that it was a double-yolked egg. The dialogue continued:

"You noticed that was a double-yolked egg."

"Yes, I did."

"Well, I kinda think you owe me another knitting needle."

In the days when Town Meetings in Vermont were inclined to be more expansively deliberative than they are now, and often more personal, a gentleman arose and informed the Moderator that he had a few questions.

"First, Mr. Moderator, if you will turn to page twenty-one of the Town Report—I want to ask if I am correct in saying that it cost the town one hundred and twenty-five dollars for Mary Brown to have her illegitimate baby?"

The Moderator looked at page twenty-one and allowed as how his questioner was correct.

"Then second, Mr. Moderator, if you look on page eighteen— Is it true to say that the town collected one hundred and fifty dollars from the young man who admitted to being the father of the child?"

The Moderator agreed that was also correct.

"Then my third question, Mr. Moderator. Is it true that the town made a profit of twenty-five dollars on this deal?"

"Well," said the Moderator, "I suppose you could put it that way."

"All right then, Mr. Moderator, my fourth and final question is: Don't you think it might pay the town to breed her again?"

Last Christmas an old-timer from Beaver Meadow came into the Norwich post office with a large gift package for his son in California. Informed of what the first-class postage would be, he was shocked, "Holy god, what's happened?" he asked.

Told that he could send it fourth class for less money, he finally settled for that, and the clerk, in good Norwich fashion, put the stamps on the parcel herself. He asked what he owed her and she repeated the amount.

"Is that all I owe you?"

"That's what I told you," said the clerk.

"Well now, that's fine," he said. "I was afraid there'd be a charge for all that spit you used."

An affluent couple from Iowa were touring the Green Mountains and persuaded a farmer in Plymouth to show them around Calvin Coolidge's lovely little hill town.

They apparently appreciated their guide's local knowledge and his wit, and the Iowan, impressed with what seemed the poverty of the area, pressed a very generous gift on him at parting, adding, "And now there is one more question I'd like to ask. How in Heaven's name do you folks in this barren neck of the woods make both ends meet?"

"Yes," said the farmer, "it *is* hard sledding a good part of the time. I don't know what I'd do without a little income from those Iowa farm mortgages."

Restraint

Economy is an old-line watchword in Yankee hill-country. We have considered thrift-economy in things material, and the same frugality is applied in the areas of language and of displaying emotion. Sometimes it is hard to tell from his words or his deportment whether a native Vermonter has just come into five thousand dollars or lost a wife.

Some years ago I told some Vermont quips and stories to the New England Society of New York at a very swank club on Park Avenue. A lady from the audience greeted me after the talk and said she wished she had heard it thirty years ago.

When I asked why thirty years she replied, "Because I have been married to a Vermonter for thirty years and it has been hell."

I murmured something about its not having been *that* bad, certainly.

"Of course it really hasn't," she conceded. "My husband is a high-minded Christian gentleman, but when he says, 'Well, if you really want to go, we will,' that marks enthusiasm. Everything scales down from that!"

52

One memorable afternoon in October 1924 I drove over alone to Plymouth Notch and in walking up to the cheese factory saw the President's father, Colonel John Coolidge, scything the grass around some apple trees. There was not another soul in sight anywhere, so I got over the fence and introduced myself. I said I didn't want to interrupt his work, but he said it was time to take a rest and, hanging the scythe over a limb, he invited me to sit down.

We enjoyed what may be called a quiet and deliberate conversation with many pauses, covering the weather, town affairs, roads and horses and sheep and suchlike. Nothing was said about son Calvin, but as I was rising to go I commented on how strange it seemed for us two to be sitting under an apple tree in Plymouth on that lovely autumn afternoon and him with a son in the White House. After a pause he said, "It does seem strange."

And then after a longer pause he added only these words: "One thing I'll say. Calvin'll never be hasty."

There are lots of Coolidge stories, some true and many not so authentic, but one I can report as told me by the gentleman who succeeded Mr. Coolidge in the Governor's chair in Massachusetts. Mr. Cox said that Mr. Coolidge had told him that being Governor of Massachusetts was not a bad job—not too time-consuming, and so on—but Mr. Cox had found himself putting in very long hours.

Meeting Mr. Coolidge at dinner one evening he remarked about this, and Mr. Coolidge's answer was: "Yes, you talk back."

Another Coolidge story (which I cannot vouch for but which is one of the more persistent ones) concerns a lady who was to sit next to Mr. Coolidge at dinner and had made a bet with a friend that she would get him to say more than two words. Telling him about her bet, she received his reaction—in two words: "You lose."

Along with emotional restraint there might be mentioned a physical endurance that is somehow related, but different. It is often apparent in the daily lives of old-line Yankees, and can take the form of a stoicism which, in this day of automatic self-dosing with painkillers and tranquilizers, astounds the doctors. I don't happen to associate much with medical men but once in a while I pick up a yarn. Like these:

There's a young internist at the big clinic in Hanover, New Hampshire, who came from the Deep South to the North Country knowing only, as he told me, that it was inhabited by damyankees. The very first patient who walked through his office door was from Royalton, across the Connecticut. Perspiration stood out on his brow, his face was blue and his hands were trembling. The doctor suspected at once that he had coronary trouble, and an examination disclosed that indeed he was in critical condition. He was told that he'd have to stay right there in the hospital. But when the doctor went over to his desk to make some notes the old man headed for the door.

"Hold on, sir!" said the young doctor. "Didn't you hear me say that you were in critical condition and would have to stay right here?"

"Yes, Doc, I did. But I'm an old-line Vermonter and goddammit I've got to go home and think this over for a week."

The same doctor told me that he later had another such old-timer in bed in the hospital and asked him one morning how he felt.

"Doc, I feel scrampopolous."

"That's a new word for me," said the young medic. "I don't know what it means."

"Neither do I, Doc; but damn it, that's the way I feel."

A doctor who is on the staff of the Veterans' Hospital in White River Junction added another story to my collection, this one about a patient from Bethel who was having trouble with his stomach. It became necessary for the man to swallow a device on a tube which would take a sample of stomach fluid. It is not a very pleasant procedure, but the patient co-operated in fine fashion, and a satisfactory sampling was obtained.

After the doctor got the device hauled up he said, "There now, sir, that wasn't too bad was it?"

"Well, Doc," the old fellow replied, "it's nothing I'd run up hill after."

At a Vermont trial a witness gave a familiar name, and the judge inquired if there hadn't been another witness of the same name that morning.

"Yes, Your Honor, he's my father."

Then from the back of the courtroom came a voice: "Well, Judge, that's been disputed."

It is not inappropriate that what is sometimes said to be the shortest known charge to a jury came from the lips of a Vermont judge in a paternity case. The arguments had dragged on for a long spell and His weary Honor evidently saw no need for lengthy disquisition on the law or the jury's duty. His charge was to the point:

"Members of the jury, this young woman says this young man is the father of her child. He says he isn't.

"If you think she knows more about it than he does, find him guilty.

"If you think he knows more about it than she does, find him Not Guilty.

"Proceed."

New Englanders have for many years entertained New York City children as "adopted summer guests." A ghetto boy gave this description of some aspects of living conditions in *his* Vermont farm home:

"You know, they have a nice bathroom upstairs, but they don't use it except when they're sick or sometimes to take a bath, and for the toilet they 'go out back.' We all took a bath in the brook and when we got ready to eat we all washed up at the kitchen sink. Gee, we didn't mind at all."

When asked what they talked about when they ate meals at the kitchen table he replied with real discernment, "When they eat they don't talk, they just eat."

A Vermont clergyman began to eat a plate of hash without saying grace. When his wife remarked on his omission, he answered, "Blessed it once already."

You can't expect much of an open response from a real back-country audience, and when, after I'd finished a talk at East Barnard, an old gentleman with a long face said to me, " 'Twas good," I took it as high praise indeed.

Some seventy-five years ago Samuel Langhorne Clemens came to Brattleboro to give one of his famous humorous lectures. According to the story the response was not what "Mark Twain" thought it should be. He stopped talking a little ahead of schedule, went out the stage entrance and around front to see if he could find out what the trouble was, and is reported to have found out in short order.

Out came a nice old couple who had driven down from their hill farm with the horse and buggy, and he heard the old gentleman say to his wife, "Wan't he funny? Wan't he *funny!* I had all I could do to keep from laughing."

Political & Otherwise

Stephen Arnold Douglas, the "Little Giant" who was born in Brandon in 1813, is reported to have said in later life:

"Vermont is the most glorious spot on the face of the globe for a man to be born in—provided he emigrates when he is very young."

And Dorothy Canfield Fisher told us that her godfather, also born in Vermont but later a long-term resident of Kansas, once suggested that the Green Mountain State ought to be turned into a kind of National Park, preserved with buildings and customs, people and habits, just as they are, so that "the rest of the country could come and see how their grandparents lived."

Which reminds us of that Congressional resolution offered by the Georgia delegation in the early 1850's, recalled by Ralph Nading Hill in his *Contrary Country*—a resolution that reflected the bitter antislavery fight in which Vermont took a very active part. The Georgia proposal called upon New Hampshire's only President, Franklin Pierce, to employ a sufficient number of able-bodied Irishmen to dig a ditch around the State of Vermont and float "the thing" out into the Atlantic Ocean.

When re-apportionment of the Vermont legislature added to my district a part of a neighboring town, I thought I should do a little campaigning there. One evening I stopped at an old house to leave my card and give my pitch, and in leaving inquired the location of the parsonage, remarking that I'd like to be sure the Lord was on my side.

With a twinkle in her eye the elderly lady of the house retorted, "Might be better to make sure you're on the Lord's side!"

Arthur Simpson of Lyndonville, both intelligent and very independent-minded, an historian, farmer and cattle dealer, long-time devoted public servant and lively member of the legislature, some years ago ran in the Republican primary for the gubernatorial nomination—and lost. The campaign enriched the fund of political anecdotes about Arthur, though, and one of my favorites concerns a friend who asked him how the race looked to be going.

"Judging by the bumper-stickers," Arthur gave judicious reply, "Ausable Chasm seems to be leading."

One evening at the home of a friend, Vermont's Poet Laureate Robert Frost and Professor Thomas Reed Powell, a native Vermonter and for many years a distinguished Professor of Constitutional Law at the Harvard Law School, were engaged in friendly chaffing and banter which both enjoyed, each trying to outwit the other.

Powell, recalling Frost's birth in San Francisco, said "You know, Robert, you're only a bastard Vermonter."

To which Frost countered: "Well, Reed, isn't that better than being a Vermont bastard?"

I used this story once on the Dartmouth College radio station (WDCR) on a "Let's Help" program, and was interrupted by one of the students involved who reported that a lady on Occum Ridge had just telephoned in to deplore the fact that Professor Foley had used the term "bastard" not *once* but *twice* on the air, and had added her sad query, "What is this country coming to?"

I explained to the young man that "bastard" was a perfectly proper word, even found sometimes in sober works of history; and that furthermore this particular story had all the earmarks of authenticity, having been attested to separately by two ladies who were present on the occasion. A few days later another lady friend of mine told me she had heard I was having a little trouble because of my use of the term "bastard," and she told me the following story—which, as she pointed out—suggests that unlovely term without using the word.

61

A good old Vermont Democrat was being chided by a Republican friend for being damned narrow-minded and party-minded.

"Pliny," his friend charged him, "I don't suppose you'd vote for a Republican no matter how fine a man he was."

"Nope," said the Democrat, "I wouldn't. The Democratic Party has a long tradition of support in my family, and in my family tradition counts.

"You see, for three generations we've been Democrats, and I'm a Democrat.

"For three generations we've been farmers, and I'm a farmer.

"And for three generations none of us has ever been married, and by god, I'm a bachelor!"

An old-time North Country farmer who was, as you would expect, a stout Republican, went to report a theft to the county sheriff, who strangely enough happened to be a Democrat.

"Yes, Sheriff," he said, "yesterday I butchered a hog and left it hanging by the barn. During the night someone came along and stole half that hog. And I'm sorry to say I think it was a Republican."

"And why," asked the sheriff, "do you think it was a Republican?"

"Because," said the farmer, "if it had been a damned Democrat he'd have taken the whole hog."

A Vermonter prominent in the Republican political machine some years ago was belaboring Austin and Aiken and Flanders and Prouty and Gibson, and throwing in Lodge and Saltonstall and Margaret Chase Smith for good measure. He was damning the United Nations and the excess-profits tax and all deals other than the good old deal.

When reminded in a half-joking way that the only trouble with him was that he hadn't had a new thought since William McKinley's day the old gentleman banged the table and countered:

"And what the hell, sir, is wrong with William McKinley?"

Years ago in a relatively small Green Mountain community, a few Democrats decided to make the highly irregular move of holding a Democratic meeting, and issued an invitation to the public. The town minister was a stanch Republican, but he had a Democrat in his congregation and he decided to attend as an observer to find out what was going on. There being no other clergyman present he was asked if he would open the meeting with prayer.

He said he was sorry, but he would have to decline. "To be frank," he explained, "I'd rather the good Lord didn't know I was here."

Back in the days when Vermont was pretty much a one-party state the Board of Civil Authority in a small town was busy counting the ballots in a state election. *Republican—Republican—Republican* seemed to run on without end until suddenly up came a *Democrat* ballot.

They passed it up and down the table, looked it all over, smelt of it, and then put it by itself in a separate place. The *Republican* run started again and went on until, lo and behold, a second *Democrat* ballot showed. As they gave it the same close scrutiny and put it aside with the first one, a member of the Board analyzed the trend:

"By god, the bastard must have voted twice."

A Vermonter took a job as a private and more or less personal secretary to President Franklin Roosevelt. On the occasion of his first visit home to Northfield he wondered what the local reaction would be.

Walking down the street he encountered one of his boyhood friends, who said to him. "Hear you're in Washington now."

"Yes I am," said the secretary. "Working in the White House. And by the way—what did the boys around here say when they heard I was working for F.D.R.?"

"Oh," said his friend, "they just laughed."

Forty or fifty years ago a very cultured and intelligent friend of mine from Thetford ran for the legislature on the Democratic ticket; needless to say he was not elected.

I should explain that the gentleman had been a Christian missionary to Japan and while serving there had been converted to Buddhism. He had returned to Thetford and on a lovely little knoll in the Pompanoosuc valley had erected a Buddhist temple, brought over a couple of Japanese monks, and proceeded there in the Vermont hills to exemplify Buddha's Golden Path. After the election I was talking with another citizen of Thetford, an old-guard Republican, and expressed some regret that my friend had not been elected.

"Do you think he would have been a good man for the legislature?" he asked with much surprise.

"Yes," said I. "I think he would have been well worthy of the office, a man as the constitution prescribes 'of wisdom and virtue.' He is well educated, much traveled, and with ethical values and a broad understanding of human nature. I think he would have been a fresh wind blowing in the Vermont legislature—though of course I know he's a Buddhist."

"Yes," said the old-timer, "I think he is a good man, and I wouldn't have minded voting for a Buddhist. But god, I couldn't bring myself to vote for a Democrat."

Back in the 1930's an effort was being made by some Dartmouth College boys to stir up an interest in *The Daily Worker,* and they had distributed some free copies of this Communist sheet. An old native of Wilder who worked on campus in Hanover was looking it over and when asked what he was reading, replied:

"Don't know just what it is. Some students want me to subscribe, but I don't think I will; get two papers now. Good reading though, and sure does pan Roosevelt. Looks like a good Republican paper."

In the mid-1940's Harry S. Truman was not a great hero in Vermont, and naturally became the butt of many stories. Shortly after he assumed the Presidency an old farmer in Vergennes was asked what he thought of him.

"Don't think much of him," was the answer. "Fact is, he reminds me a good deal of my Uncle Charlie."

"What do you mean by that?" he was asked.

"Well now, that's right: I guess you didn't know Uncle Charlie. He was sort of the black sheep of the family, and not overbright. Years ago he went down to Philadelphia. He got a job down there, a job playing the piano in a house of ill-repute.

"And I'll bet he played that piano for two years before he had the slightest idea what was going on upstairs."

I can't vouch for this story, but it was certainly popular in Vermont in the late 1940's. According to the usual version, President Truman liked to go fishing down off Key West, and on one occasion fell overboard. Three American sailors at once came to his rescue and later in the day the President had the three lined up on deck in order that he might show his gratitude for their prompt action. Mr. Truman said that to show his appreciation he would be glad to do anything within the power of the Presidency, and, turning to the first sailor he asked, "What can the President do for you?"

The young man replied that he had always hoped to go to the U.S. Naval Academy at Annapolis. Mr. Truman was delighted at this and said he would see that he had a Presidential appointment to the Academy.

When asked what the President could do for him, the second sailor expressed a desire to go to West Point.

And Mr. Truman promised a Presidential appointment to the U.S. Military Academy.

Then, turning to the third sailor, he asked what he would like the President to do for him. This last young man seemed shy and embarrassed, but finally managed to stammer out, "I think, Mr. President, what I would like is a first-class funeral with full military honors."

"What do you mean," said the President, "at your sunrise time of life, asking for a funeral?"

"Well," said the sailor, "you wouldn't know, sir, but I come from Vermont. And when I get home and they find out what I have done, that's what I'll be needing."

Officials who in many states are called assessors, in Vermont are called "listers." We had a lister bill in the legislature which made it legal for a town, if it wished and so voted, to elect as one of the three listers a citizen who was not a resident. The idea was to get once in a while some outside wisdom and advice as sort of a check. It was to be optional with each town and seemed to me a good idea.

I was walking out after the session when an old member from down-state said to me, "I noticed you voted Yes on that lister bill."

"Yes I did," I admitted.

"Why'd you vote Yes?" he queried.

I explained my thoughts on the matter—that it was optional, that sometimes I thought an outside judgment was helpful, etc., etc.

"Yes," said he, "I know that; but my town's not going to like it."

"Well," I told him, "then they don't have to do anything about it."

"I know. But my town don't like to have other towns permitted to do what they don't want to do."

This same legislator came into the House one morning complaining that he was terribly tired. I asked him if there was any special reason why he should be so tired and he replied:

"Oh, Lord, I don't know. I guess it's just because the Democrats are in.

"You know, I never got tired like this when Calvin Coolidge was President."

A political contemporary of Mr. Coolidge's told me of one day when he and two others were with Mr. Coolidge for an entire day of campaigning in eastern Massachusetts in the course of which the taciturn

Vermonter said practically nothing to him or to the others.

When they came to a small town where they were scheduled to talk with a few Republican leaders Mr. Coolidge spoke three words, "Where's the hotel?" He went to the hotel, bought a newspaper, and settled himself behind it in the lobby until it was time to move on to the next town.

One of my constituents once said to me, "Foley, I like you but I don't understand you."

"Why's that?" I asked.

"You don't vote right "

"You know we are living in 1965," I told him, "and you cannot turn back the clock."

"I know that," he replied; "and damn it, I've found sometimes you can't even stop it."

I heard of the summer visitor in a small Champlain valley community who was surprised to note one native with whom the other natives had little or nothing to do, although the man certainly seemed to be normal and respectable. Eventually curiosity got the better of him and he asked one of the local residents whom he had gotten to know fairly well to explain the reason. The friend was reluctant, but after much urging finally admitted that this particular person was something of an outcast.

"Well, you see," he explained, "he's a-spending of his principal."

At a convention of veterinarians in Vermont I heard of
the salesman who was off in the back-country trying to
sell tractors. As he drove along he saw an old farmer in
the field plowing with a bull for power, and thought this
was his chance. He waited until the farmer got down to
his end of the field, snapped the bull whip and turned
back for another furrow. Then he started his sales talk.
The old-timer showed absolutely no interest in a tractor,

and finally allowed as how he already had one—safely stowed away under the barn. Whereupon the salesman attempted to argue that he was foolish not to be using it instead of the bull, and got this reply:

"Mister, this is the best way I know to show the damned bull that life ain't all romance!"

Vermont and Texas are the only two states that were independent republics before they joined the Union—Vermont for about fourteen years (1777—1791) and Texas for about nine (1836—1845). Their years of autonomy did something for both of them, and, though there's not much traveling back and forth by natives of the Green Mountains and the Lone Star State, occasionally the two different lifestyles meet eyeball to eyeball with results such as these . . .

A fellow from near St. Albans was visiting a friend outside Lubbock when he spied a very bright-plumaged bird beside the road.

"What bird's that?" he asked.

"That," replied the Texan, "is a bird of paradise."

"I'll be damned," said the Vermonter. "Long way from home ain't he?"

Back in the days when Texas was pretty straight Democratic—as Vermont used to be solid Republican—this same visitor from the North Country was taken to a dinner meeting of a sportsmen's club. Talk sooner or later got around to politics, and the chairman, knowing there was a guest from Vermont, decided to have a little fun in the lull while tables were being cleared.

Rapping on his glass for attention, he announced: "Will all those who are Democrats please stand up?" All but the Vermonter got to their feet.

"Thank you," the chairman said. "You may be seated. Now if there is a stray Republican present, will he please stand?" Amid good-natured laughter the visitor rose.

"Would you tell us, my friend, how it happens you're a Republican?" asked the chairman.

"I'd be glad to," said the Vermonter. "Two reasons only. In the first place I come from Vermont. And in the second place my father was Republican before me."

"That is a very poor reason for being a Republican," the Texan said, "a very poor reason indeed. Suppose your father had been a horse thief?"

"I reckon in that case," replied the Vermonter, "I'd been a Democrat!"

I heard of another visiting Vermonter who was being reminded by a Texan host of the vast difference in the size of the two states.

"Why," said the Texan, gleaming with local pride, "there's hardly a county in Texas in which Vermont couldn't be put down and still have a lot of land left over."

"Offhand," replied the Vermonter, "I can't think of a county in Texas but would profit by having Vermont put down in it."

One fine summer day in 1967 in Montpelier I saw a Texas car parked by the curb and waited around to see if I might meet the Texan. Sure enough, it wasn't long before he showed up big as life. In the course of the conversation he remarked how small our state was, admitted it was a beautiful day, and then for some reason said we seemed to have a lot of damn fools in Vermont. I agreed we had *some*, but maybe a no larger proportion than they had in Texas. He allowed as how that probably was so, and went on record that one of the Texas damn fools was in the White House.

He then told me that he had wanted to see a real, old-time family farm—not a show place into which a city fellow had put a lot of money, but a genuine Vermont hill farm. He said a friend in Montpelier had taken him to such a place, where he had met the farmer. I gathered that part of the conversation had gone like this:

"Glad to meet you," said the Texan. "Nice place you got here; quite a farm. How much land you got?"

"Pretty good-sized farm for around here—'bout two hundred acres."

"Where I come from that's a piddling small place, if you don't mind my saying so," remarked the visitor. "Down in Texas I drive for most of the morning before I get to the corner of my ranch."

"Ayeh," the old-timer commiserated, "I had a car like that once, but I got rid of it."

Some years ago a young fellow from the Northeast Kingdom who had just finished his legal training decided that advancement would be rather slow in his home town, and was drawn to the idea of going to Texas, passing the bar exam there, and hanging up his shingle in a fast-growing Southwestern community. He wrote to the Bar Association of Texas, therefore, to ask what his chances might be, and concluded his letter with the statement, "I am an honest lawyer and a Republican."

The Texas Bar Association replied promptly and with encouragement: "Come on out. You should do well in the practice of law in Texas: we can always use an honest lawyer, and as a Republican you would be protected by our game laws."

Before direct dialing came to Vermont a Texan staying in St. Albans expressed shock when told the charge for a telephone call he'd made to Brattleboro, diagonally down to the opposite corner of the state.

"Why, man," he told the hotel clerk, "in Texas for that money we could make a call to hell and back again!"

"But in Texas, sir," the clerk asked gently, "wouldn't that be viewed as a local call?"

And there's the story about a man from Quechee who, late in the afternoon in the North Station in Boston, was taking a train to come back to White River Junction. The train was crowded and a well-dressed city man sat down beside him. After getting acquainted the Bostonian said:

"You say you are just a Vermont farmer, but I am

much impressed with your general intelligence and common sense. To pass the time I suggest we play a little game."

"Well, what's your game?"

"I suggest we each ask the other a question, and if we can't answer the other fellow's question we give him a dollar."

"Well now, that might be a good game. But I don't think the terms quite fair."

"What's wrong with the terms?"

"Well, you're a city man, probably well educated and traveled. I'm just a poor Vermont farmer—only went through grammar school, and spent all the rest of my life on the farm. So I suggest that if you can't answer *my* question you give *me* a dollar, but if I can't answer *your* question I give *you* fifty cents."

"That seems fair enough. Let's play. You ask the first question."

"Well, I'd like to know what it is that has three legs and flies."

After some thought the city man said, "Damned if I know. Here's your dollar."

"All right," said the Vermonter, "what's your question?"

"I'd like to know *what it is* that has three legs and flies."

"Damned if I know. Here's your fifty cents."

...& Four for the Road

A Middlebury man who dealt in horses let it be known that he had a fine pair of blacks for sale, and in due time a Boston lover of fine horses called to see the pair and said he was interested.

Said the dealer, "You've been a good customer of mine for years, and though some say there's no sentiment in a hoss trade, I say there can be. I'll sell you this pair at a special price—three thousand dollars."

After some thought the Boston man replied, "By god, there *is* sentiment in a horse trade. To prove it, I'll pay you more than the blacks are worth—three hundred dollars."

"Well," said the Vermonter rather deliberately, "it's a hell of a discount. But the hosses are yours!"

A salesman for government bonds during World War II went canvassing deep in the North Country, and up in the hills of Vershire one day he came to an old farmhouse where he saw no roadside mailbox, and no utility poles that would indicate contact with the outside world. Out in the barn he found the farmer,

who was said to be "a bit deaf." The encounter went something like this:

"Hello. I'm selling government bonds."

The old fellow just shook his head.

"You know there's a war on," in a louder tone.

The farmer looked up at the haymow and shook his head again.

"You must have heard of the trouble at Pearl Harbor."

Again the old man shook his head.

"You know about Roosevelt and Churchill."

Again the response was negative. The salesman gave up.

When the farmer went back to the house his wife asked, "Who was that man? What did he want?"

"Don't know exactly," the old-timer allowed. "But it seems some feller by the name of Rosyfelt got Pearl Harper in trouble over on the Church Hill, and wanted me to go his bond."

At the time the Vermont legislature was discussing the adoption of the Nineteenth Amendment to the Constitution of the United States, which gave women the vote, Senator George Aiken's father happened to be a member of the House. Mr. Aiken, who favored the extension of suffrage to women, was being interrogated by a member who opposed this move: "Mr. Aiken, you say you favor this amendment."

"Yes, I do."

"You realize, Mr. Aiken, that if we give women the vote we'll have to give them all the other privileges of full citizenship."

"Yes, I do."

"You realize, Mr. Aiken, that this will include jury duty."

"Yes, I do."

"Well, Mr. Aiken, suppose in a criminal case that runs on for four, five or six days your wife was the only woman on the jury and had to be closely confined with those men during all this period. How would you like that, Mr. Aiken?"

"I think," mused Mr. Aiken, after carefully studying

the big chandelier in the center of the hall, "I think it would all depend on who we had for a hired girl at the time."

We have all had a passing remark strike home. My most recent experience of this sort occurred while I was chatting with a seventy-year-old neighbor in Norwich.

"D'you know what my next assignment is?" he asked me.

"No," I said, "I don't."

Said he: "It's to retire from retirement."

What the Old-Timer Said

The above is the title for the sampling* of quips
and stories I've run into during a half-century of
forays into Vermont back-country, and the little
book seems to have yielded pleasure to more folks
than I ever imagined would see it. It has brought
funny, friendly, and I may say, enthusiastic responses not only from all over America, but also
from England, France, Spain, and even Japan.
Many of the letters were from Americans in residence there, some native Vermonters or with Vermont connections. These people are apparently
glad to be reminded of a way of life that has somehow uniquely characterized our North Country.

*The first 80 pages of this *opus*, as originally published in 1971.

You recall the old-timer's statement that just because the cat gave birth to her kittens in the oven doesn't mean that they're biscuits. Place of birth, I have the firm notion, doesn't absolutely brand us with an indelible mark.

If the truth must be known, I was born in Massachusetts, about a month before the signing of the treaty ending the Spanish-American War, and I was educated in the schools of Framingham and at Dartmouth College, just across the Connecticut River from Norwich, Vermont. I spent long summers during student days in Maine at Tenants Harbor, devoted a happy year to the study of history at the University of Wisconsin, one more as an instructor at Dartmouth, and three at Harvard. This was followed by a gloriously leisurely trip around the world which, through the kindness of friends, was at no cost to me. Why I was so lucky, I'll never know.

Returning from that trip I rejoined the Dartmouth faculty and some years later, in 1941, took up residence in Norwich. This was just a few months before the Pearl Harbor holocaust. I've been in Norwich ever since.

But I get ahead of my story. W. C. Fields used to say that when he was born folks came for miles around to take a look: they weren't sure just what the little thing was. Happily I was not quite in that class, but—unlikely though that may seem to people who know me today—I was a puny child and folks wondered how long I would survive.

It was because of this early sickliness that the Green Mountain State entered my life, because as boys my younger brother and I were sent for a number of summers—in that blessed period before World War I—to spend several weeks at the farm of Uncle Charlie and Aunt Mary in Newark. Charlie and Mary weren't really related to us, being old friends of my mother's family, and they certainly gave us as boys a wonderful taste of old-time country living.

I remember there were cows on that farm and what must have been a fairly gentle bull. There were pigs and horses, both for work and riding, and a hard-working dog, and the inevitable cats. The dog was hard-working because there were lots of sheep to keep in line, and there were two rams which, as I remember, operated the small treadmill that ran the machinery used in separating the milk and churning butter.

Strange things stand out in a long memory. We drove occasionally to Lyndonville, and one day Uncle Charlie took us to Vail Manor, now incorporated into Lyndon College but then the country place of Theodore N. Vail, at that time the president of American Tel & Tel. Although the family were not in residence we were shown through the house, and I remember the twin towers and a secret staircase and especially a throne-like seat over Mr. Vail's private toilet—he was a large man as I recall—with the inscription

HERE I TAKE SOLID COMFORT

For some reason I remember, too, an early buggy ride. The family were in two buggies, I in the second one with Aunt Mary, and as we were

83

going toward Burke Hollow Uncle Charlie came running back toward us in high excitement, waving his arms. What had happened was that Charlie had met an automobile on the road, a Maxwell roadster I think, and was coming back to help us get by. Automobiles were that rare then. He got the buggy well over to the side of the road and held the horse's bridle firmly while the car chugged slowly by. Charlie was civil to the driver and thanked him for his help. But he let go when the car had disappeared in a cloud of dust.

"Damn 'em!" he said, or something to that effect. "They can have those contraptions in the city if they want to. But why in the devil do they invade God's country?"

It wasn't so many years after this that I was back, boning up on some Latin in the Clark School in Hanover and living with Sherm Somerville's family on their farm out on the turnpike in Norwich. It was good to be in Vermont again, and it was a pleasant summer with good progress toward an exam for Latin credits for admission to college. Sherm was quite a character, and I picked up a lot of expressions from him. One I find myself using every now and again: "Talk's cheap; but damn it, it takes money to buy rum!"

In the Fall of 1916 I entered Dartmouth as a freshman. Even undergraduates travelled in those distant days by train and disembarked at the old Norwich-Hanover station in Norwich. There was usually horse-drawn transportation across the Connecticut river bridge into Hanover, but most of us walked up West Wheelock Street to town—a climb more often than not referred to as "that goddam hill."

Happily, Vermont was not out-of-bounds, and we hiked through her back-country a lot in those days. Often on Saturday afternoons we'd walk down the railroad tracks on the Vermont side, stopping once in a while to play a game of duck-on-the-rock, or visiting at a well-established hobo camp. We'd get a meal at the old Junction House (now Hotel Coolidge), perhaps stir up a little hell in White Town, then walk back to Hanover on the New Hampshire side, sometimes singing vigorously.

I know that all this sounds simple-minded to the undergraduate of today. But as Charles Dana Gibson once said, reminiscing about his happy youth, "If I remember correctly, we had a pretty good time then too."

A few of us got acquainted with the station agent upriver at Pompanoosuc, the next train stop north of Norwich, and at times we headed that way. Harry, the agent, was then a bachelor, and his mother kept house for him in what had been the old station across the tracks from the new one. She would always say, "You boys must stay for supper" —and we always did. And though she might say she really didn't have much to offer we'd always sit down to a table of good victuals and plenty of them. Then we'd sit around and talk and listen to the old Edison phonograph.

Towards nine o'clock Harry would remind us that the way-freight would be coming down pretty soon. We'd go over to the dark little station, where Harry would get his lantern and flag the engineer down. We all piled into the cab, visited with the engine crew on the way south, and when the train slowed down for the Norwich station we'd hop off. It was probably a violation of the rules, but no one ever came to harm and we had fun.

Then there were the so-called "deputation trips" when three or four undergraduates went

out to spend a weekend in some small community. A visit to Bradford sticks in my mind. There were two co-operating churches across the street from each other, one Congregational and the other Methodist. Contrary to what you might expect, the Methodist preacher was a jolly fellow and the Congregationalist was a serious-minded sober man. At the Sunday evening service they planned to take up a collection to pay for our train fare, which was the only cash involved in the entire weekend. The meeting was held in the Congregational Church, but the Congregational minister said he would rather not be the one to ask for the collection since his Methodist brother had "a way about such things." The Methodist agreed to do it, but warned his Congregational brother that he would do it in his own fashion.

After stating what the purpose of the collection was, and how much the community had enjoyed having these Dartmouth boys here with us, he closed his appeal by saying, "My eyesight is not too good, but Brother Alexander has eyes like a hawk, especially when watching the collection plate, and God help the person who doesn't put in at least a quarter."

Well, as I said, I travelled around a bit after leaving college, learning a little history and something about teaching it. I recall three sticky summers in New York City where I taught at Columbia. Finally I was back in Dartmouth and World War II was upon us.

It was during the war, when I was going from St. Johnsbury to Swanton on the old St. J. & L.C. Railroad, that I found myself sitting in the baggage car next to O. W. M. Sprague, a professor at the Harvard Business School. We were in the baggage car, I remember, because the small passenger section was full, and they'd placed rocking chairs for us where we could look out the open car door and admire the wonderful sweep back to the White Mountains.

The Professor, I remember, knew a great deal about the building and financing of this railroad some seventy years earlier, and he told how the company used camp-meeting methods, with music and entertainment preceeding the pitch for support, to raise money from the towns along the proposed route. The Professor told me he had found a partial press account of the chief promoter's talk given in the big tent specially erected at Hardwick. It ran something like this:

> "Ladies and gentlemen of Hardwick, we appreciate your attendance today and I want to make one last appeal for your support. Remember that this part of the railroad line is to be part of a projected trans-continental line of communication. The first step is to connect Portland, Maine, with Ogdensburg, New York, on the St. Lawrence River. Then through the Great Lakes we will hook on to a trans-continental line through to the Pacific Ocean, and by ship be open to the trade of the Far East.
>
> "Think, my friends! The town of Hardwick will then be directly connected with the fabled lands of China and Japan. Keep in mind the thrill which will be yours as you look up from your haying some fine summer day and see the express train go by: You'll catch a whiff of the private tea-stock of Queen Victoria being rushed from the tea fields of China direct to Windsor Castle."

When I retired from Dartmouth in June of 1964, my neighbors in Norwich sent me to the House of Representatives in Montpelier to represent the town. Decorum in that House, I found, is pretty impressive, and that's as it should be. But there are a couple of incidents I will pass along to you.

One year we had a bill dealing with the inoculation of dogs against rabies. It was a simple bill, and with a favorable committee report it should have breezed through the House without delay. But there are always members who suddenly get the urge to talk, and there was a lady so moved on this occasion who was recognized by the Speaker.

She first expressed her conviction that there were too many dogs in Vermont, elaborating rather fully on her feeling. Her next point was that the wrong people had dogs; and, while some might agree with this position, it had nothing to do with the bill at hand. Her third point dealt with the fact that dogs either by instinct or training or both always did their business in the neighbor's yard. She said that when she came out of the house, unless she was very careful, she'd put her foot in it. And when she tried to cut her lawn with a power-mower she got an unwelcome shower-bath.

The trouble with this kind of talk is that it invariably lures others to their feet. The member

from Poultney took the floor when the lady was through and inquired if something was wrong with the previous speaker. Didn't she know what a dog could mean in the life of a boy? "And," he added, "I want to tell the members of this House that a well-trained dog will behave in the house as well, if not better, than a well-trained child." The member from Craftsbury then took the floor to make a sharp rebuttal: "The trouble with the last speaker, Mr. Speaker, is that perhaps he doesn't realize that to train a dog you've got to know more than the dog does."

Then a usually dignified member from Montpelier put his oar in. "Mr. Speaker, I have a solution to at least one of the lady member's worries. That is, to put britches on the bitches." And so it continued until a member from Brattleboro suggested we call it quits, with an entry in the House Journal that this was the day when "the House went to the dogs."

The House of 1973 included an unusually large percentage of young members. A member from Bennington, aged 25, was responsible not only for an excellent move but one that also brought a lively laugh from the members. It concerned a somewhat foolish resolution designed to make Vermont's Dairy Queen the State Hostess of the year.

Resolutions, it should be explained parenthetically, may be offered by any member, and, without consultation or consideration by committee, may be put to immediate vote of the House. Or, by motion, a resolution may be treated as a bill and referred to an appropriate committee for consideration; without such consideration, however, the House is likely to vote favorably on resolutions, be they good, bad or indifferent.

The young member from Bennington rose and spoke as follows:

"Mr. Speaker, I am opposed to this resolution and opposed in principle to such beauty contests in general. They degrade womanhood. You put nice girls on parade before a big crowd—sometimes a leering crowd—and judge their appearance in an unseemly fashion. It's like a cattle show. I therefore move, Mr. Speaker, that this resolution be treated as a bill and referred to the Committee on Agriculture."

By a loud affirmative voice vote of the House, it was so referred, and there, happily, it died.

Another story has to do with State symbols. Vermont has some fine ones—the sugar maple is the state tree and the Morgan horse the state animal, etc. The trouble seemed to be that Vermont does not have a state rock. A lady member proposed a bill which would give that honor to a rock called green schist. Now green schist is plentiful in Vermont. It can be frequently seen along road-cuts on the new interstate throughways, where it takes on a lovely soft green color when wet.

Probably the only drawback to adopting green schist as the state stone is that its name must always be pronounced, to avoid misunderstanding, with great care and clarity.

The wags were soon on their feet. One member observed that it was a good choice because there was so much of it in Vermont. Another favored the suggestion because it was so easily picked up along the roadside. A third questioned the choice because Vermont would then have to be known as the Green Schist State. After more of the same, the matter was referred back to the committee for further study. If memory serves, we never heard about the matter again.

The Judiciary Committee of the House had under consideration a bill the purpose of which was to reduce what was viewed by some as large-scale and objectionable nudity in certain areas of the state, including what is known as skinny-dipping. At lunch one day I asked a member of that committee what the committee was going to do with that bill. He replied in a semi-confidential tone, "I doubt if that even sees the light of day." Whereupon a long-time member who was sitting with us commented, "Well now, it's all right after dark anyway."

The Vermont Senate is a notably dignified body —most of the time. But I recall one Windsor County senator who spoke in favor of a bill to allow farmers living in the back-country to place small signs on the main roads to advertise their produce to the traveller. He pointed out how helpful and even essential such signs were, both for seller and buyer. And especially, he said, in the case of remote farms almost impossible for the stranger to locate. He knew of one such farm in Windsor County, the senator observed, so remote that they had to keep their own tom cat.

Well, tom cats are way off the subject. What I started to say was that my earlier book, WHAT THE OLD-TIMER SAID, seems to have amused and pleased quite a few people. In view of this unexpected response I have tried to collect here a few more little stories in the modest hope that these, too, may give pleasure.

Contrary Country

Very often there's sound advice in an old-timer's response to no matter how routine a question.

A friend of mine asked an old fellow, "How are you today?"

"God," was the reply, "I think I'm pretty good—unless you want to go into de-tails."

Last mud season my friend Will Atwood, driving me into Montpelier from Adamant, was reminded of the following story. I'm afraid I can't vouch for its truth.

Silas Smith, hopping across the flat in mud-time, spied Heber Brown's hat. So Silas reached out with a pitchfork and very, very carefully lifted the hat: and there was Heber, up to his ears in mud.

"Heber," observed Silas, "you're really in it."

"I'm OK," Heber replied. "But the team's in pretty deep."

There was no doubt about it that it was Heber Brown's son, Alfred, who got Ira's daughter into a peck of trouble. The fact is she was in a family way. So Ira went to talk to Heber about it.

As it happened, Heber wasn't there so Ira spoke to the hired girl instead. She tried to be helpful.

"I know Heber gets twenty-five dollars for the bull," she explained. "I don't know what he gets for Alfred."

An old-timer surprised me the other day with this:

"A bunch of us boys was sitting round the stove in Sam's store the other night, the way we have for years, talking about our neighbors and half-joking sometimes about each other.

"So I up and said: 'Do you know what we ought to call these sittin's? Well, if it was in the city, they'd be called group therapy sessions, and we'd be paying twenty-five dollars an hour for the treatment."

An out-of-state visitor with gourmet tastes stopped at a little restaurant in the northern part of the state. The elderly female proprietor came tottering in to ask what he wanted.

"Do you have frogs' legs?" the customer asked.

"Nope," replied the old lady. "I guess it's just my arthuritis."

Direction jokes are part of the landscape in our part of the world. Joel Carew at Dartmouth College used to tell this one, one of the best I think. To spare feelings, I've changed the name of the town.

A motorist came to a fork in a Vermont road. As usual, there was no sign to guide him.

"Which way to South Tinbrook?" he asked the aged countryman who was sitting on a nearby front porch. The man pointed toward the south road.

"Is it far?" the visitor asked.

"No, but when you get there you might wish it was a sight further."

A friend told me the other day about an experience he had driving back up into the hills of Windsor County on a windy winter's day. The dirt road not only led sharply uphill, but it curved and was desperately narrow.

Finally my friend reached the farmhouse and settled down in the kitchen to visit with the old fellow who lived there alone, a dog curled up at his feet and a cat purring by the stove. The visitor remarked about the steep and narrow road, and said it might be pretty bad if you met anyone coming the other way.

"Nonsense," replied the old gentleman; "nothing bad about meeting somebody on the road. It's the passing that's makes the trouble."

An old-timer named Wallace Gilpin, long since departed this world, used to publish a weekly paper called the *Orleans County Monitor*. It was a small-size, four-page sheet with an annual subscription price of one dollar. Wallace did just about all the work himself—gathered the news and ads, set the type, and ran it off on his little press.

The neighbors tended to be slow in paying up their subscription bills and every once in a while Wallace would go out collecting. One day he arrived in his Model T at a farm whose owner owed him for three years' back subscription. Their conversation went something like this:

> Wallace: "Well, Joel, I thought I'd see if I could collect some of the subscription money you owe me."
>
> Joel: "I'm sorry, Wallace, but I ain't got a damn cent."
>
> Wallace: "Couldn't spare me a dollar, Joel?"
>
> Joel: "Nope; I told you I ain't got a cent."
>
> Wallace: "Well, how about a nice little pig?"
>
> Joel: "Ain't got a pig on the place."
>
> Wallace: "What about a roasting chicken?"
>
> Joel: "Nope, no roasting chickens."

Wallace, disgusted, made one last try.

> Wallace: "Now, Joel, you wouldn't have a bag of nice clean corncobs, would you?"
>
> Joel: "Nope, I ain't got no corncobs. Why in hell do you think I keep subscribing to your paper?"

A small church in Addison County had gotten rather shabby, badly in need of painting and general refurbishing. The congregation decided to purchase the necessary materials and enlist contributions and volunteer labor from the village.

It all worked out well: the building was painted inside and out, the floors were sanded and polished, the pews were refinished, some of the electric fixtures were replaced. Even the lawn was improved.

Later the congregation arranged a get-together to express appreciation to all who had helped. The chairman of the Improvement Committee singled out major contributors and special workers, and paid tribute to each and all. When he appeared to have reached the end of his list a little old lady rose and spoke as follows:

"This is all very good and we do appreciate these improvements. But nothing has been said about the manure we put on the lawn. I want you to know that came through me."

The late June flood of 1973—the worst in Vermont in some forty years—fouled some of the local water supplies. In Norwich, for example, we were advised not to drink the town water for a while unless we boiled it first.

A friend of mine, some days later, called the Town Clerk to ask if it was safe now to drink town water. The response, in genuine old-timer style, was only:

"Nope. They're still biling."

Caleb was inclined at times, like some others we know, to take too much to drink. His wife, Mary, labored with him patiently and at long last, after about thirty years, he seemed to have gone over pretty well to the side of abstinence.

Then one night after an encounter with some cronies, Caleb came home no longer sober. Mary, disappointed and angry, finally said, "You're not to sleep in this house tonight, Caleb Jones. Grab yourself a blanket and go out to the barn." He went.

Along about three in the morning Mary roused from her sleep, reached over on her husband's side of the bed, and then suddenly remembered her rough treatment of Caleb. Remorseful that she had kept him out of his own house after thirty years together, she got up, lit the lantern, and went out to find him.

Mary expected to find him in the horse barn, but he wasn't there. She tried the cow barn: no Caleb. She couldn't believe he'd bed down with the pigs—but there she found him, sound asleep next to a friendly sow.

Presently he stirred in his sleep, turned toward the old sow and began running his hand along her belly. And as Mary waited in the corner she heard him mutter, "Mary, old gal, didn't remember you had so many buttons on front of your nightgown."

Weston Sayre, who used to live up the mountain back of Jericho, would came down to Burlington twice a year, and while there on one visit was side-swiped by the car of a tourist and knocked down. The visitor, frightened and solicitious, jumped from the vehicle and asked Sayre if he was hurt.

"Well," replied Weston, "it ain't done me much good."

This is an old, old story out of Orange County. A countryman was driving down to the village early one morning when he saw hanging from a limb of a tree near the road a fellow from a neighboring town who was not too well liked. On arriving in the village, the old-timer spied a friend and told him what he'd seen.

"God, Link," asked his friend, "didn't you cut him down?"

"Nope," was the level reply: "he was still a-twitchin'."

An old-timer who used to trap up in Essex County a good part of each year was asked if he'd ever been lost in the woods.

"Not lost, no. But I was awful bewildered for two days once."

Here's a story told by Admiral William S. Sims. It was during World War I when Sims and a couple of friends were staying overnight at the old St. Johnsbury house. Those were the days when a Vermont breakfast was a major undertaking, and the waitress rattled off a long list of tempting dishes, then added, "You can have 'em all if you want."

Sims and one of his friends contented themselves with bacon and eggs. But the third man in the party said he'd have the whole list—except for the apple pie.

"Land o' goodness," said the waitress. "What's wrong with our apple pie?"

Sims, on a tour of duty later in England, would often tell the story there. More than once, he reported, someone from the British audience would came up to him afterwards and ask: "By the way, Admiral, what *was* wrong with that apple pie?"

And of course you all remember the Bennington horse trader that was approached by the dude.

"What do you want for that mare?" the young man asked.

"I'll take a hundred and a half for her," the trader said. "But she don't look so good."

They discussed the pros and cons of the animal and finally reached agreement. The new owner paid and went off with his purchase.

He was back again the next day, mad as hops.

"What's the matter with that horse?" he demanded to know. "She ran me right off the road."

"Been blind for a year," the Benningtonian admitted. "Told you she didn't look so good."

Habit of Thrift

Some fifty years ago a couple named Brougham lived in what the maps call West Norwich but which is known locally as Beaver Meadow. The old man liked to chew tobacco, and when he'd gotten the goodness out of a chew he'd roll up the cud neatly and put it on the back of the kitchen stove to dry out.

Well, the old lady—and this is a true story—liked to smoke an old clay pipe. She would take the dryest cud at the back of the row, loosten it up a bit in her hand, then pack it into her pipe. It smoked right well, she claimed.

Now, this is not only a perfect example of rock-ribbed thrift; it also warms the heart of this old teacher, who has always claimed that history, in its strange fashion, does repeat itself. For Mrs. Brougham was anticipating by half a century one of our pet projects today: recycling.

A retired professor who now has a year-round place near Lake Fairlee reports this story.

A New York City family bought an old farm near by and proposed to fix it up in first-class style. They had a deed for 150 acres of land and thought that first they'd have the land surveyed and the boundary lines located. They wanted an

A-1 survey that would stand up in any court, and in their ignorance they figured that no surveyor in a little rural State could be relied on. So they brought a high-powered team of three civil engineers up from New York, at a cost which you can imagine.

They got on well with the survey except for one corner which they could not seem to locate. Seeing an elderly farmer swinging a scythe in a nearby field, they told him their problem and asked if he could help. The old-timer allowed as how perhaps he could, particularly as they promised to pay if he could locate this one corner.

So he started off, walked about a tenth of a mile, got down in some scrub growth, poked around a bit and then called out, "Here's your corner." The engineers agreed it was the one they were looking for. They thanked him for his help and handed him a card with their New York address, suggesting that if he would send them his bill they would see he was paid. A week or so later he mailed them a bill for a hundred dollars.

They replied that they were glad to hear from him and, although they rather felt his charge was excessive, they would pay it if he sent them an itemized accounting.

In due course it came: "$25 for finding the corner, $75 for knowing where it was."

We are all familiar with the innocent-seeming stickers that decorate the windows of unsold cars in dealer showrooms. They start out with a "basic price" for the car. But then there follows a number of built-in items, such as power steering, undercoating, bumper guards, etc., that alter the total price, usually out of all recognition. In this story, you will be happy to know, the tables are turned.

For by a strange fluke of fate a local car dealer one day appeared at Perley Moore's hill farm wanting to buy a cow. Farmer Moore showed the dealer to the barn and told him to pick out an animal. The dealer examined the herd keenly, made his choice, and asked the price.

"That's a one-hundred-dollar cow," Moore replied without hesitation.

"Very reasonable," said the city man. "I'll take her."

"That's the basic price," Moore added, getting out a stub of pencil. "There are one or two extras of course." He did some figuring on a piece of paper, handed it to the dealer. This is what he had written:

Basic cow	$100.00
Two-toned exterior	45.00
Extra stomach	75.00
Storage compartment and dispensing device	60.00
Four spigots @ $10 each	40.00
Genuine cowhide upholstery	75.00
Dual horns @ $7.50 each	15.00
Automatic fly-swatter	35.00
Total:	$445.00

Mrs. Tolby, who lived for years in a small house directly on the river north of Hanover, had a woodlot and after the death of her husband, hired her wood cut by a neighbor. He'd half filled the woodshed by nightfall one cold November day, so she asked him in for a glass of whiskey.

The old-timer finished his drink before commenting: "There was no such thing when I was a young 'un."

"Whatever do you mean?" asked the widow. "No whiskey?"

"Plenty of whiskey," he answered. "Never in such a small glass."

I'm indebted to Ed Mead, writer and Hanover, New Hampshire, neighbor, for an ancient story, a true one as far as I know, about an old farmer who stopped at the Tilton ticket office, back when it was still called Sanbornton Bridge. This is New Hampshire, mind you.

"How much to Littleton?" he asked the ticket agent.

"Two dollars."

The farmer said nothing for a bit. "Well then, how much for a cow?"

"Three dollars."

"A pig?"

"One dollar."

"Book me as a pig," said the old-timer promptly.

Town History

A couple from New Jersey were telling about their first winter in Londonderry. It was late in the year when they closed the deal for the house, but they decided to make the best of it and spend their first winter without central heat. A friendly neighbor warned that the cellar walls were laid up roughly with many chinks, and advised banking the house.

My down-country friends said they were well enough off financially with a good mortgage. But their neighbor explained that he wasn't talking about money but about putting up a little fence around the cellar walls and filling up the space to block the drafts. You could use sawdust or leaves or hay for this purpose, he told them, but probably the best insulation was cow manure. So he helped put up a fence and they banked the house with manure.

Just before the first snow came, the couple were visited by a lady friend from New Jersey, and she naturally wanted to know what all that mess was around the edge of the building. They explained. The visitor said she was going to enjoy telling this story to friends back home. Just as she was leaving, she asked a final question.

"But how in the world did you get all those cows to back up around the house?"

Walter Needham, historian of Guilford and co-author of that wonderful time-capsule of a Vermont classic, *A Book of Country Things,* tells of the founding of the Retreat, Brattleboro's pioneering mental hospital, something like this:

Richard Whitney, a lawyer of Guilford, seemed to be talking a little peculiar—this was way back at the start of the last century—so the doctors held him under water a while, as had been done to the Salem witches, then revived him.

Whitney still talked funny, so they put him back under the water—for a little longer this time. Still no improvement in Whitney's ways. So they kept at it in the same progressive fashion until finally he wouldn't revive at all.

Mrs. Anna Marsh, who had observed all this and didn't like it, left some money to be used for the mentally afflicted in Windham County, and that, they say, is how the Retreat got its start.

"Whitney," Walter reports, "is buried over in Hinsdale, and doctors have been using hydrotherapy ever since—with somewhat happier results of late."

Herbert Haskell, who had farmed well his acres on the Dover-Wilmington road, in his later years would oblige a neighbor or a proper-seeming transplant by sharpening shears or setting saws. When Jenny Evans was three years old and extremely tiny even for this early age, her father, Bol Evans, took her with him to visit Haskell and ask the old gentleman if he'd sharpen some mower blades.

After the usual amount of fore-talk, and the business concluded, Evans introduced his daughter, who was standing shyly near by. Mr. Haskell studied the diminutive girl a moment, then commented:

"Y' almost didn't get your seed back."

As that loyal Vermonter, Sheldon Dimick, tells it, he was being shown over an old house that was up for sale. It was full of hundreds of empty beer and whiskey bottles. They were in every room, filled every closet.

The old lady showing Sheldon around commented on this. He asked her:

"Do you mean to say the man who lived here drank all that himself?"

"Oh yes," she said. "He was a bad man. But the drink finally caught up with him."

"How old was he when he died?"

"Ninety-three."

Some years ago a storekeeper in Danville had two new cast-iron stoves come in from the manufacturer, and remembering that a customer down in Peacham had ordered one, he put the stove on his old pung and drove down some seven or eight miles to deliver it. It was a below-zero winter day in the North Country and, as he said, "It was a damn long, cold ride."

When the dealer arrived he set the stove up and started a fire to show it was in good working order. Unfortunately the sudden heat was too much for the cold iron. The stove cracked and split.

Although the dealer should have known better, he at least was resourceful: he drove back to the store, started a fire in the second stove, put it on the pung and drove all the way back to Peacham with a boy riding along to keep it stoked.

The old-timer remarked, "By god, Jeb, the boy kept warm even if you didn't."

A newcomer to town, a college man and all that, bought quite a piece of land, and was planning a very ecological-minded lumber operation.

But the natives found him peculiar: they couldn't get over the fact he always seemed to wear overalls and farm boots, a flannel shirt and a tattered straw hat. Sometimes he even had a piece of hay in his mouth.

"I don't know as there's anything really wrong with him," Old Will said judiciously one day down at the store. "He dresses like that 'cause he wants to look just like what city folks think we look like."

Mrs. Neil Malone, daughter of the Vermont attorney and author, Thomas Reed Powell, has told me some good stories about her family. Some have appeared in *What the Old-timer Said*. Now I'd like to pass a couple more along to you.

One her father liked was of the stranger who stopped by at the County courthouse in a small town in the Green Mountains and asked to speak to the Clerk of Court. The janitor told him he was over at the barber shop.

"When will he return?" inquired the stranger.

After taking good aim at the spittoon, the janitor replied, "When he's finished there."

The stranger explained that he had important business and must see him, and received the stern reply:

"Mister, you don't seem to know much about how we do things in our part of the country. What be your name?"

"Charles Evans Hughes, Chief Justice of the Supreme Court."

On her father's twenty-first birthday, Mrs. Malone says, Grandpa gave him a beautiful gold pocket watch. His presentation speech, in full, was as follows:

"Son, we'd always planned to give you a watch when you reached the age of wisdom. We've decided it's better not to wait."

Streaking, at the time of this writing, has not enlivened the Vermont scene to the degree experienced in some other states. But there have been a few demonstrations, including this one:

In a small town an elderly couple, both around 70, appeared one warm day trudging down Main Street clad only in shoes and, in the case of the man of the house, hat and necktie.

"My god," said a friend upon meeting them, "are you two streaking?"

"Nope," said the wife, "too old to streak. We're snailing."

Speaking of rocks, one old-timer was working in his Wardsboro garden when what the late Frederic Van der Water has dubbed a permanent summer resident stopped by and commented:

"You got a lot of rocks in that garden, haven't you?"

"Most two rocks to every dirt," was the reply.

A philosopher countryman has declared:

"I like a rock or two in a garden. Gives me something to tap my hoe on."

Comeback

Time was when city folk tended to underrate the old-timer, holding that wit and wisdom and such things originate in the city. A friend in Colchester was telling me the other day about two down-country types that spied an old gentleman at that endless occupation of New England hill farmers, digging the rocks out of his field (what the forms from Washington call "obstruction removal.")

The two city men stopped to have a little fun with the farmer. "What are you doing?" one of them asked.

"Picking stone," the farmer replied, going on with his work.

"Where did they all come from?"

The farmer still didn't look at them. "Glacier brought 'em," he replied.

"Where'd the glacier go?"

The farmer slowly stood up, and took a long look at the city men.

"Back to get some more stones," he said.

A gentleman named Eddy was summering on Lake Willoughby up north in Orleans County. He went into the Town Clerk's office in Westmore to ask if he could get a fishing license.

The elderly clerk, busy writing at a table, didn't look up from his writing, but answered, "Yes, take a chair."

Some time elapsed while the clerk continued his writing and Mr. Eddy, somewhat impatient, stated his request again and added, "I happen to be President of Chatham College in Pittsburgh, Pennsylvania."

The clerk continued his writing, never looked up, and replied:

"Take two chairs then."

At a church supper in North Thetford one of the waiters was a 14-year-old boy, put to work early as many country boys still are. A lady summer visitor had finished the main course and was asked by the boy if she'd like some dessert. She said she might and inquired what they were offering for dessert.

"Pie," said the young man; "apple and mince."

"What do you recommend?" she asked.

Following good native practice and cautions, his reply was: "I don't."

A certain pretty tight-fisted farmer drove his hired hand pretty hard, and at such times as he was getting his hay crop down and dried and in the barn, along with milking and the other chores, the hired man worked pretty much from sun-up to sun-down.

One evening, after a long day's work, as he and the hired man were milking the large herd—by hand, of course—the farmer remarked, "You know, Seth, sitting here milking is kinda restful to me."

"Well, maybe," said Seth. "But I don't know but I'd ruther go to bed tired."

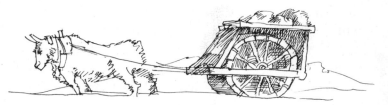

Then there was the old-timer who was getting deaf. His wife kept urging him to see a doctor: he'd know right away, she said, what could be done about it. The old man succeeded in putting his visit off for some time. But she kept after him and finally one day he found himself sitting in the doctor's office with the MD quizzing him closely:

"Jeb, do you smoke?"

"Hardly smoke at all."

"Drink?"

"Yes, well I drink a little," Jeb admitted reluctantly.

"You can't drink, you know: you've got to stop that." Pause.

"Don't think I'll do that."

The Doctor hitched his chair forward purposefully.

"Jeb," he said, "you're just going to have to quit drinking. If you don't, you'll grow stone deaf."

"Guess I'll get deaf, then," replied the old-fellow: "I like what I drink better'n what I hear."

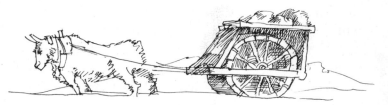

In the first years of Mount Snow, before the ski resort had achieved much in the way of commercial lodgings, an old-timer and a friend were discussing the manners of strangers from down-country who virtually demanded to be put up, money no object and willing to rough it.

"What can you say to one of these birds," the friend complained, "when they bang on your door and ask how much you'd charge to let 'em sleep out in the barn with your bull?"

"I'd say ten dollars," the old-timer said: *"My bull's registered."*

A prominent Cavendish lady was always mindful of those less fortunate in the community, and among other kind deeds always tried to invite some person outside the family, particularly someone who was alone and without relatives or friends, to share her family dinners on special days like Thanksgiving and Christmas.

One Christmas she decided to invite an eccentric handy man who could always be called on in time of need to do most anything, and who lived alone in rather squalid quarters. She met him on the street and extended her invitation. He thanked her, but said he'd have to think it over. One of his well-known peculiarities was that in the winter he would always wear several suits of long, heavy winter underwear, which he rarely changed, plus a couple of pairs of pants and several heavy shirts.

A few days later she met him again and he gave her his reply to the invitation:

"Now, Miss Gay, I thank you for your kindness, but I've been thinking it over and I just don't know. I'd have to take off all my clothes and take some kind of a bath, then try to find something else to wear. And, you know, Miss Gay, I've about decided that it ain't worth it."

It was foliage season—early October, that is—
and a tourist out cruising the back roads felt the
need for immediate toilet facilities, so he stopped
at a farm and knocked on the door. The lady of
the house, learning of his need, directed the
stranger to the privy out back. On arriving there,
he discovered to his embarrassment that it was
occupied by the farmer himself.

"No bother," said the farmer. "This is a two-
holer. Come on in."

Later, as the farmer was leaving, a dime fell
out of his pants and slipped down the hole. The
farmer got out a large leather wallet, removed a
five dollar bill, and tossed it down the hole.

"What in the world did you do that for?" the
amazed visitor exclaimed.

"Mister," said the farmer, "you don't think, do
you, I'd climb down in there for a dime?"

A young Vermonter who had studied for the ministry became pastor of a church in a lively Green Mountain town. During student days he had taken up golf, and one of his parishioners, a city man who had retired to Vermont, used to invite him to play the game occasionally.

The city fellow, despite his years, was a better golfer than the young minister, and one day when they got back to the clubhouse the preacher was feeling despondent, for he had played a particularly poor game.

"Never mind, Reverend," said his friend, "you'll have the last word. You'll probably bury me."

"Maybe," said the young man. "But it will still be your hole."

Native courtesy is often remarked on by students of the back-country—even though, more often than not, it is relieved by straight-from-the-shoulder frankness.

An undergraduate friend of mine, a stranger to the area but anxious to get acquainted with the place, was wandering around one day in Windsor County. He stopped at a little village store and asked the old proprietor if he could tell him how to get to the famous Windsor-Cornish bridge, the longest covered bridge in New England.

"Yup," replied the old-timer, giving him a hard look, "I could. But I don't know if you'd ever make it."

An old fellow up in Orleans County who had a reputation for being a shrewd man in a deal and tight-fisted to boot, had passed on to his reward, and some of his cronies were talking about the funeral coming up the next day. One suggested that the nicest thing they could do would be to put some folding money in his hand in the coffin. Another agreed to ask his son what he thought of the idea, and if he approved they'd make a collection right away.

The son, evidently a chip off the old block, agreed heartily.

"That's a great idea," he said. "You collect all the bills you can and bring them to me. I'd be glad to write a check for the amount and put it in his hand."

Sometimes we don't count our blessings here. Not so long ago, a Randolph man was visiting his brother who'd moved out to Texas with his family. Both husband and wife were working, so the Randolph man got in the habit of buying his lunch at a small restaurant around the corner. One day, getting up to go, he remarked to the owner that it looked as though they might get a little rain.

"Hope so," said the owner, peering up at the sky. "Not so much for my own sake as for the boy's. I've seen it rain."

When Gil Emmons died—it must have been fifty years ago—he left $20,000 in the savings bank, a goodly sum in those days. Although he left a will some of his heirs were not satisfied and one, who had moved to the city, contested the will and hired "a damn smart city lawyer" to plead his case. The lawyer got friends of the deceased to testify in the hope that he could get one of them to suggest that the deceased was not in his right mind at the time the will was drawn. The first witness, one Bill Cook by name, demonstrated that sometimes even back-country old-timers are a match for sophisticated city lawyers. The interrogation went something like this:

Lawyer: "Did you know Mr. Emmons?"

Cook: "Yes, knew him pretty well."

Lawyer: "Did you see much of him during the last year of his life?"

Cook (cautiously): "Yes, some."

Lawyer: "That's good." Then, pressing his advantage: "This next question is a very important one: When he was alone, did you ever hear Mr. Emmons talking to himself?"

Cook (after thought): "Come to think of it, I never was with Mr. Emmons when he was alone."

A friend of mine has a sightly summer place, up on a hill overlooking Thetford Center. An old-timer had come to do some mowing for him one day and my friend asked if he didn't think the view was nice.

"Yep," said the man, " 'tain't bad at all." Pause. "But it won't buy you no flour."

A fellow who dealt a bit in this and that once stopped at a hill-country farm and said perhaps he'd like to buy a cow. The old farmer allowed as how they were all in the barn and he'd be glad to have him look them over. The dealer picked out a good-looking animal, and after some dickering the price was settled at seventy-five dollars, which he paid. When they got the cow out to put her in the truck, the dealer discovered the animal was stone blind.

"You damn fool," he berated the farmer, "that cow's blind. I can't sell a cow that's blind!"

"Well," said the old-timer, "*I* just did."

Vermonters All

Several years ago there was a very late Spring snow that lured so many skiers to Mount Snow from down-country that the cars were bumper to bumper for more than a mile on the access road. The late Archie Fitzpatrick was in charge of winter work then, and he was plowing the heavy snow with the town truck while his two sons, William and Willard, were standing in the back of the big truck shovelling sand into the spreader as the truck moved slowly along.

Finally the skier right behind him could stand the delay no longer: he pulled out to pass the plow truck, skidded and spun around—having no snow tires—and smashed his pretty grillwork to hell and gone against the side of the truck. Furious, he got out of his car to tongue-lash Archie: "Goddam it, let me see your license!" he shouted.

Archie took a long look at the damage, shook his head and replied: "In Vermont you don't need a license to get run into."

Driving on a back road in Underhill one winter's day, a good Vermonter and a city fellow ran into one another, doing some damage to both cars. The Vermonter walked to a nearby farmhouse and phoned the state police. When he returned, he offered the city man a drink from a bottle he had in his car.

They sat in the car and chatted a while. It took some time for the officer to arrive. The city feller said he was a bit nervous. The Vermonter offered him another drink. After a good swig, the stranger asked if the Vermonter wasn't going to join him.

"Maybe wait until the police have come," the native replied honestly—"and gone."

Some years ago a grizzled farmer, tinkering with a rusty harrow on a back road in Marshfield, was accosted by a bright young man peddling a new manual on soil conservation and improved farm techniques. After explaining how helpful this manual could be, he asked if the farmer would like one. The old man replied:

"Reckon not, son. I don't farm now half as good as I know how to. Got to catch up on what I know before I take on any more ideas."

Not too many years ago, a Vermont farm boy was drafted into the U.S. Army. He was a self-respecting lad in the old tradition, and when he appeared for induction he was neatly dressed with his hair cut and his shoes shined.

The officer in charge was duly impressed, spoke kindly to the boy, and finally asked if there was anything he could do for him to make his stay in the Army a pleasant one.

"Well thank you, there is," said the boy. "When hunting season comes 'round, I'd like some time off so I can go hunting with the boys up on the mountain."

A 1924 clipping from the *Boston Herald* provided this story. The place is the little town of Reading in Windsor County, and the time is the early nineteenth century.

A storekeeper named Levi Grindle had the reputation of being more than a thrifty Vermonter: he was known as a very parsimonious man. Trudging home one day on foot, he was given a lift by one of his neighbors' small boys who was driving a farm cart. On reaching his destination Grindle took out a capacious wallet, fumbled within it, and finally produced a one-penny piece. After some hesitation he gave it to the boy.

The next day the boy, anxious to spend his penny, went into Grindle's store. Seeing a box of figs the boy picked the biggest fig he could find and tendered the penny in payment. Grindle took the fig in one hand and the penny in the other and pondered.

"Quite a lot to give for a penny," he said at last. "Dunno as I can afford it." After due reflection he raised the fig to his mouth, took a generous bite and handed back what was left to the boy, tossing the penny into the till.

"Guess that makes it about right," he said.

A late March snow one year in the Northeast Kingdom prevented the preacher from getting to a funeral in the back-country. The undertaker suggested that in view of this one of the departed's friends and neighbors might like to say a few words.

A long pause ensued. Finally an old-timer stood up and said:

"If no one has anything to say about the deceased brother, I'd like to take a few minutes about the next election."

A man named Bailey was a local captain of industry. In addition to the store he owned water-power privileges and several mills including a sawmill, a small woolen mill, and a gristmill. A neighbor named Hapgood owned several acres of land near Bailey's mills, which, for purposes of expansion, Bailey wished very much to buy. But Hapgood persistently refused to sell and a long-standing feud developed.

Hapgood was the older of the two and in failing health. To make sure that after his death Bailey never got the land he wanted, Hapgood decided to deed the area to the town for a free cemetery, with the proviso that it should never be used for any other purpose.

In due time Hapgood died and was buried in this cemetery. Then folks heard Bailey swear a mighty oath: "By God he can keep me out of the mill-site but bedamned if he can keep me out of the cemetery."

It wasn't until 29 years later that Bailey died, but two stones, only a few yards apart, proved Bailey right and bore silent testimony to the futility of feuds. The inscriptions read:

DAVID HAPGOOD. DIED 1821, AGED 72 YEARS.

LEVI BAILEY. DIED 1850, AGED 85 YEARS.

A Burlington couple had given a stained glass window to the church in memory of their dear departed parents, who had worshipped there all their lives.

Desiring a brief story of the window in the local weekly, the lady visited the editor and told him that the major theme in the window was the ascension of Jesus into Heaven as described in the last verses of Luke's Gospel.

"Oh, you should go over and see it," she added. "There is Jesus, attended by angels, going right up to Heaven with Mt. Mansfield in the background."

After forty-one years of public service to his state and the nation, and continuous service in the United States Senate since 1940, George Aiken's announcement in February of 1974 that he would not be a candidate for re-election marked the approaching end of one of the longest and most distinguished careers in Vermont's political history.

Senator Aiken is in so many ways representative of what we call the typical Vermonter that it is not surprising to find that spirit reflected in many of his down-to-earth remarks and comments. He really qualifies as an old-timer.

When asked some years ago if he and Mrs. Aiken were going to Europe that year, his reply was,

"No. Somebody's got to stay home to fill the wood box."

And in a brief letter to former Republican National Committeeman Edward Janeway the Senator explained his decision not to run again for the Senate with one laconic sentence:

"I decided the only way to get a day off was to not run for re-election."

Half these long-standing quarrels we hear about have their origins so far back that most of the time no one, not even their chief participants, remember what they were all about in the first place.

The feud—and that may be a strong word for it—between the Foster and the Chase families in what I've been told was the town of Chelsea was just such an affair as this. Aron Foster wouldn't talk to the Chases. And Bill Chase not only ignored the Fosters but forbade his family to have anything to do with any of them, even the children.

But Mrs. Chase didn't like this state of affairs. She urged her husband to forget and make up. It wasn't Christian to hold a grudge all this time, she kept telling him. She reminded him that the Chases and the Fosters had been close neighbors for years, and she spoke about the old days when the two families had got along fine and had acted as good neighbors should act.

This kind of propaganda went on for quite awhile and ultimately it had its effect. Mrs. Chase realized a thaw was in the making, and she said to her husband one Spring day:

"Bill, you know this'd be a good time to get things back to the way they used to be. Why don't you go right over to the Fosters and ask to borrow their roto-tiller, the one you used to borrow each year? Act like nothing had ever happened; act just like you used to in the old days."

Chase thought this over awhile, decided it was a good idea. So he climbed in the pickup and started over to his neighbors.

But before he got there he began thinking. Why should I borrow his old tiller, he asked himself. For heaven's sake, it wasn't as if he didn't have money in the bank to buy one for himself. Maybe Aron wouldn't want to lend it? Why *should* Aron lend it to him anyway, after all those years of silence? Suppose that instead of saying Sure, Foster just gave him a black look and said "Chase, why in hell should I let you have my tiller? What have you done for me recently?" And then I'd look pretty damn silly going back to the wife with an empty truck.

Chase thought some more: I shouldn't take the old tiller even if he pressed it on me, he thought. Probably the best thing would be to give Foster a poke right in the snoot. Why should I be insulted by that fat idiot, just because he has an old tiller he wants to get out of the yard?

At just about this stage in his thinking, Chase arrived at the Foster house. He leaped out of his truck, stomped into the house without knocking, ran into the dining room where he found all the Foster family sitting around the dining room table, looking surprised.

"Foster," he yelled, "I don't want your tiller. You can damn well keep your old tiller. I wouldn't take it if you gave it to me with a sack of turnips. I hope it digs up your best strawberry bed, that's what I hope. You and your damned tiller can go straight to hell."

Then Chase got back in his truck again and drove home, feeling a lot better.

A quotation from the *St. Louis Daily Missouri Republican* of May 27, 1843:

"The people of Vermont are celebrated the world over for morality and uprightness but we were not made aware 'till lately that even their convicted scoundrels were trustworthy.

"The *Mercury* says that a young man recently arrived at Windsor on the stage and applied for admission to the State Prison, showing the papers which entitled him to residence there.

"It seems that he had been convicted in Montpelier of some offense, sentenced to the State Prison for six months and in order to save expense was fitted out with his papers and sent on to Windsor by stage without sheriff or other attendant. On reaching Woodstock the stage by accident left him behind but he coolly waited a day and took the next stage!"

Apropos the recent flood, *The Rutland Herald* published a letter from a former Vermonter who described himself as "transplanted in the desert Southwest," and who recalled the remark of an old farmer during a flood some years earlier:

"I was going to pick some peas for lunch. Now I guess somebody downriver in Connecticut will get them."

Some stories about Calvin Coolidge are true and some are not, and it often becomes difficult to verify the difference. A gentleman in Northampton, Massachusetts, told me this yarn and thinks it is authentic.

You know Mr. and Mrs. Coolidge lived in Northampton most of their adult lives, retired there after their stay in the White House, and Calvin died there.

One morning in that period of retirement, Mr. Coolidge went down to his favorite barbershop for a haircut. The only other customer in the shop at the time was Mr. Coolidge's Northampton physician. Nothing was said between the two men until at one point the doctor turned toward Calvin and asked:

"Mr. President, are you taking the pills I prescribed for you?"

Calvin's terse reply was, "Yes."

The doctor's haircut was finished first. He got on his coat, paid his bill and left the shop. When Calvin got ready to leave, he seemed to be going without paying up. Said the barber, "Mr. Coolidge, I think you are forgetting to pay for your haircut."

"Oh, yes," replied Calvin Coolidge, "I was so busy talking with the doctor I must have forgot."

President Coolidge always tried to spend as much time as possible with his father, Colonel John Coolidge, at the old homestead in Plymouth. During one of these visits his father, who was on the board of directors of the bank in Ludlow, said he should attend a meeting of the board that evening. The President said he would drive him down.

When they arrived some of the directors were visiting outside the bank and Calvin got out of the car with his father and greeted them all. When it came time to go into the meeting, he took his leave with the remark, "Some directors direct: some don't."

President Hoover once remarked to Coolidge that he couldn't understand why his recovery programs had not yet produced results and why his critics were howling so loud.

Coolidge replied, "You can't expect to see calves running the field the day after you put the bull to the cows."

"No," replied Hoover, "But I would expect to see the cows contented."

It was in those dimly but happily remembered days before inflation when old Mrs. Black died "on the town," and the town fathers got Reuben to dig the grave. He dug a nice grave, they planted Mrs. Black, and Reuben put in his bill for ten dollars. The selectmen wouldn't pay it and the question came up in Town Meeting. Reuben put in a powerful plea and wound up with a game-winning clincher:

"By god, I'm going to get ten dollars—or up she comes."

And while we're on the subject of graves, Walter Hard tells the story about the sexton who had managed to hang on to his gravedigger's job for a number of years, but had never been regarded as a model of industry.

A day came when the head of the cemetery association felt a talk was in order.

"Jeb, I don't like to speak of this but it seems to all of us on the committee that each grave you dig is a little shallower than the one before. Can't have that, you know."

"You ain't seen anyone climb out of any of them yet, have you?"

The Old-Timer
Will Tell You

That neighbors can be good friends, but it won't pay to be *too* neighborly.

That travel may broaden a man's horizon, but staying home and taking care of the farm puts more in his pocket.

That a dog may be man's best friend, but a good cow is more help at the table.

That Californians like to brag about their weather, but they never have a chance to really appreciate beautiful days the way we do in Vermont—when occasionally we get one.

That while we are told that we can't get along with women but can't get along without them, there often can be middle ground.

That the passing of a good friend, like the felling of a giant pine, leaves a vacant space against the sky.

That "Moonlight and Roses" is a good subject for a song, but sunlight and a good ear of corn does more for the stomach.

That it's nice to sit and think but sometimes it's nicer just to sit.

That what you don't say won't ever hurt you.

That independence is better than riches.

That you can't always judge a cow by her looks.

That if you don't know the difference between east and west, you don't know much.

That silence is golden.

That it's better to wear out than to rust out.

I Want to Thank

these inspired reporters and story-tellers for their generosity: Will Atwood, Roland Boyden, William A. Carter, Sheldon Dimick, Janet Greene, Ralph Nading Hill, Mrs. Neil Malone, Edgar T. Mead, Walter R. Needham, Marguerite Hurrey Wolf. And I'm grateful to my gifted illustrator, John Devaney, for his being so consistently funny: I hope one day to be able to thank him in person.

A. R. F.